DATE DUE

FEB 0 5 2010	
FEB 0 6 2012	

A Tempest Tale

Rough Magic

CARYL CUDE MULLIN

Second Story Press

Library and Archives Canada Cataloguing in Publication

Mullin, Caryl Cude

Rough magic / by Caryl Cude Mullin.

ISBN 978-1-897187-63-0

I. Title.

PS8576.U433R68 2009   jC813'.6   C2009-903081-0

Edited by Kathy Stinson
Copyedited by Kathryn White
Cover and text design by Melissa Kaita
Cover photo by istockphoto

Printed and bound in Canada

Second Story Press gratefully acknowledges the support of the Ontario Arts Council and the Canada Council for the Arts for our publishing program. We acknowledge the financial support of the Government of Canada through the Book Publishing Industry Development Program.

Published by
SECOND STORY PRESS
20 Maud Street, Suite 401
Toronto, Ontario, Canada
M5V 2M5
www.secondstorypress.ca

For Camryn, my own dragon girl, and for Riley,
who works her gentle magic on me every day.

Act One

Materia Prima

I.i.

She stared into the brazier. A powdery mold of dead gray ashes lay in its base, but nothing else. It was a cold morning, and the servant was slow to arrive with the coals for her fire. Hunkering lower under her blanket didn't help much. It was thin. She was thin. Even when she bundled it around herself, it didn't make her very warm. She chewed her lip and frowned. "I'll have the servant beaten for being so slow," she said. She didn't really mean it. It was something she would do, if she was a grown-up princess. She was only five. No one listened to her. "What's the use of being a princess anyway," she muttered. One day they'd obey her. Not like now. "They always come to me last," she grumbled.

She was right about that. If she'd been born a boy, things would be different. But she was next to useless as an heir. "The spare," she'd heard them call her. They didn't mind that she heard them say it, either. They'd smile, and sometimes ruffle her hair. She was a pretty child, so they indulged her. She could have made a favored plaything of herself, but she hated them. Stupid them.

She grew colder and crosser with each passing minute. The shuffling sounds of the servants moving down the hall annoyed her. They were bringing coals and warm water to other rooms. It was deep winter. The world was old and flat and empty, and they'd left her here alone. Where was her nurse? Probably off giggling with that guard. They thought she didn't notice, but she did. She noticed everything. "Stupid, stupid," she repeated, this time aloud. "I'll show them all." And she glared at the charred dust of past fires lying in the brazier, making them her enemy, making them the servant to be beaten. Then, in the midst of her anger, she found a quiet place inside her that said, *I know what to do.*

Everything she needed was inside her. The thought of fire joined the word, and her will brought them into being. In a breath of spoken air, the power blossomed out from her and became what she wanted.

She stared into the dancing flames. They seemed watery, somehow. Pale. She willed them to be stronger, warmer. It was not enough. There was something she was missing. She frowned, her tongue poking past her lips in concentration. Of course. It was because of the ashes. The fire needed better meat to feed upon. She sifted the remnants in the brazier with her mind. The ashes held distant memories of the trees they once were. These coals had been olive branches, pruned to hold the vigor of the tree in its core.

For an instant, she was within its wood. She felt squeezed,

trapped. A dark shadow passed over her thoughts. There was a warning in this, something she did not understand. But she was not a fearful child. With a twist, she wrenched her mind free and pulled the memory forward into being once again.

The brazier was filled with plump burning coals. The fire snapped and ate greedily, rich now in warmth. She smiled, pleased with herself, and basked in her new comfort. "That's better," she said. Her voice unraveled itself in her room. She remembered that she was still alone. What an idiotic nurse she had. Someone should have seen how clever she was. Then she y... ...leep itself cradle her. The flames dwindled down and the coals glowed quietly in their common, tame fashion.

～

It was not much later when a servant hurried in, apologies and gossip bubbling from her lips. The queen had had a baby in the night. A boy, but it was sickly and the whole house was in an uproar. The servant was amazed to discover the princess sleeping contentedly by a warm brazier, her head resting in her arms and a smile on her lips. The servant was puzzled, but shrugged. The princess must have called out to someone else to make her fire after waiting so long. Oh well. She dumped her load of coals onto the pile already there. No one else needed them, not at this late hour. She pursed her lips and made a small snap of displeasure. It was shameful that the child had been left alone like this. She left to find the girl's nurse.

I.ii.

Every day for a week after that Sycorax lit her own fire in the morning. She looked forward to waking up and making the flames dance. It always took a handful of courage, because each day she had to face the grinding panic of calling forth the wood for the coals. But the rest of it was easy, glorious. Now she could change the colors of the flames, too. The fire was a toy.

But no one saw her new game. No one paid her any attention at all, anymore. They were all in a lather over her new brother. She couldn't see why. "He's going to die anyway," she said to her nurse.

"Hush now, don't say such evil," her nurse gasped, horror all over her face like the grease from her supper. Nurse always smelled like roast lamb. It made Sycorax's nose twitch. She supposed that the silly guard must like the sheepy stink. He certainly grinned a great deal whenever he saw them.

"It isn't evil, it's the truth," she retorted. "I see it in the fire every morning. He doesn't belong here. He was made for the next world. Only strong people can live here. Like me," she added proudly.

Nurse stopped brushing her hair and grasped her by the shoulders. "What is this that you are saying, child? Be true now, no tales here. Do you see what is to come in the fire's light?"

Sycorax tried to shift away from her nurse's hold, but the woman gripped her forcefully. "Only the morning fire," she said sulkily. "Only in the fire that I make, when the flames come and dance. They show me." Sycorax grinned tightly over her small sharp teeth. "They show me lots of things," she added.

Her nurse stepped away from her, staring. Sycorax still smiled, tasting the woman's fear. *Now she knows I'm a princess*, she thought. But it wasn't so much fun, really, to be looked at like that. As though she was something horrible. And then her nurse turned and ran from the room.

Sycorax was afraid, then. Would she get in trouble, real trouble, for saying the baby would die? It was true. She shouldn't be punished for saying the truth. But she remembered the time she called her aunt a swine, and her nurse had hit her with the hairbrush many times for saying so. That was true, too. Her aunt was always eating and grunted softly whenever she had to sit or rise. "Piggy, piggy," she said now, to make herself brave.

There were voices in the corridor. Above them she heard the shrilling of her nurse, but there were men's voices too. Sycorax twisted her skirt in her hands, but otherwise did not move. She was a princess. They could not hurt her.

The room filled with people. She recognized some of them.

They were her father's wizards. One of them, a great wide dark-bearded man, crouched down before her and stared into her eyes. "Your nurse has been telling us odd tales," he said, calmly, with a smile on his lips. He was curious, but she could see his doubting thoughts.

The others had encircled them, and together they poked at her with their minds. She didn't like it and pushed them away. The high wizard before her fell back on his heels. The rest began to babble and gasp. One of the women cried. Her white doughy face crumpled up and got all blotchy. Sycorax stared at the red spots on the woman's face, at the tears flowing over her wobbly cheeks. She'd never seen a grown-up person cry before. It made her look like a child. "Stop that," she said. And the woman stopped crying. She had no choice.

The youngest wizard, a man who had just stopped being a boy, ran out of the room. She knew that he was running to her father. Sycorax thought that she had never seen anything so funny as the sight of his bare feet slapping on the floor. He was so flustered that he didn't even notice his shoes had fallen off. Not by accident, though. She'd made it happen. She wondered what else she could do.

Her life was utterly changed. Everyone noticed her now. The wizards came each morning to watch her make the fire, to hear what she saw in the flame. Her father, the king, sent for her every day. She would stand in the throne room and people would bow to her. Her nurse's guard friend never grinned at her anymore. He stared straight ahead, like a statue. He was afraid of her.

The whole castle was in such a state about her power that

they hardly noticed when the small brother died, slipping quietly away from the ties of life. His mother keened, but she was mostly alone in her grief. She was only a second wife, anyway. They didn't need her anymore. King Aedes had married her so that he could have a son. But he didn't need a son anymore, either. It was too bad that the boy had died, but he'd been ill from birth. Not like the princess. Most powerful magic user ever, they whispered, and thanked the gods for such a protector.

That's what she was now. A protector. She liked it. She liked being important. The other wizards tried to teach her, but she already knew everything. They soon had to learn from her. They had to work and sweat in their spellcasting. Not her. "She breathes magic," she heard one of them say. "We are truly blessed."

She never told them everything that she saw in the fire, though. She didn't understand most of it. She kept seeing her father. He was old, unkempt, crazed. She only told them the good things she saw. The rich harvests. The city they would build. They would smile, and praise her.

But her nurse suspected something. "Tell me what else you see," she asked, one night when they were alone.

"I don't know what you mean," Sycorax replied, and turned away in her bed.

The nurse didn't ask again. She pulled the blanket, the new, thicker blanket, up over the girl. "Sleep well," she said.

The next day the nurse died. It was a funny accident. She slipped and fell down some stairs.

Sycorax did not know what to feel, but now she was truly alone.

I.iii.

The feasting had gone on for three days now. Sycorax was tired of it. "I can't wait until it's over," she kept saying to her husband.

Stamos smiled at her patiently every time. He was fifteen years older than she was, his soft, thin hair graying, wisdom etched in every line of his face. The news of their engagement had been greeted with a mixture of surprise and humor. Publically he was heralded as a rock of stability, but she saw through the empty diplomacy. He was the third son of a smaller house. In the past people would stare blankly when his name was mentioned. It had never been mentioned very often. Their betrothal had led to a panicked maneuvering of alliances. Everyone wanted to catch the favor of the new Prince Consort.

He seemed oblivious to the social uproar around him. She liked him for that. He was a small hollow of calm ground on a plain ravaged by whirlwinds.

But even that was not why she had married him. She chose

him because he was kind. It wasn't a learned kindness, either. It was the fabric of his soul. It was all he knew how to be. It was her fervent, secret hope that he would lead her onto a better path than the one that haunted her visions. The one that ended with her complete despair.

He smoothed the tension from her forehead. "Keep frowning like that and you'll be as furrowed as I am in no time," he teased. "Enjoy yourself. You've earned this reward. Your father is strong, his throne secure, the land is safe and prosperous, the people admire you."

"The people admire my father. They're terrified of me. And I didn't miss you calling yourself my 'reward.'"

He grinned and pulled on a loose lock of her hair. Stamos knew how to take her words lightly. "They're still grateful for the party. You should be as well. You're eighteen years old, married to a pillar of wisdom, and your long happy life is stretched out before you."

His words were a statement, but she knew they held a question. It was the same question behind every pair of eyes that ever looked into her own.

What will become of me?

She might be only eighteen years old, but for thirteen years she had been facing and ignoring the same desperate plea. It had left her jaded. Six years ago when a courtier asked her to read his fortune she had barked, "You will live. And when you are done with that, you will die." No one had ever asked her the question since, but it was still there, faltering on the tip of every tongue.

She brushed it away. "I thought I married a man, not a pillar," she said. Her words stumbled. It was a poor joke.

"Lucky woman, you have both," he said, and nibbled at her neck in a way that irritated her even while it made her laugh. She let him swallow her up in an embrace.

～

The celebrations did end, in time. Sycorax grew accustomed to Stamos' quiet shadow in the corner of her life. She reminded herself that she ought to be happy. Her country had been at peace for so long, a generation. Her father's people had become comfortable, even prosperous. Buildings were springing up that celebrated architecture rather than fortification.

Her spells had made the country so, and kept it so. But it was a gem whose gleam was now perceived and valued from afar. Rulers of distant empires rubbed their avaricious hands and increased their armies. The name of her land began to appear on maps that once had left it unmarked and overlooked.

Sycorax was not afraid of any of them. Her power was greater than any army. But she would have to be ruthless to keep them out, and she knew that making such magics, even as a defense, would poison her soul.

She knew it from experience, though no one guessed. She was the Wizard Royal, the Great Protectoress, the Heir Apparent.

Murderer is what the flames called her.

Sycorax shook her head and turned her thoughts away. She

would write her own fate. A wave of fatigue swept over her. That had been growing more common lately. "It's only natural," the physicians told her. "You'll need to rest so the child within you grows strong."

Child. Sycorax pulled back her shoulders and stood straighter. She didn't know how to be a mother. The whole idea was faintly ridiculous, though she was the only one who seemed to think so. The birth of an heir was a great comfort to her father and her people.

Sycorax's own mother had died bringing her into the world. She wasn't worried about that. There were simple magics that any wise woman could do. Herbs and water and soothing words were all that were needed. Her foolish mother had been afraid of magic and had banished it from the birthroom. So the queen had perished, while Sycorax lived, wizardry in her bones.

Sycorax rubbed her swollen abdomen. It was a daughter that grew inside her. She refused to see beyond that. When the morning flames tried to show her more, she snuffed them away. It was a foolishness of her own, no doubt. Knowledge was a tool. *A weapon*, whispered an imp in her mind. She wouldn't listen to that either.

"I protect my people," she said aloud. Her voice was harsh, rasping. She had been silent too long, alone too long. Stamos was somewhere nearby; she felt his anxiety slithering under the door like an autumn draft. She was keeping him away. He was so pleased about the child. "I'll be a father!" he had crowed. So ignorant and naive, like a child with a new toy sword announcing he is going to war.

Did he not realize that his child would also be hers?

"I protect my people," she whispered again.

Her father – old, blind, mad, decrepit – sitting on a crumbling throne.

Sycorax shook her head again and began to walk around the room. The rhythm of her steps brought quiet to her mind.

Stamos would worry if he saw her. He didn't like it when she paced like a beast in a cage.

I.iv.

Stamos named the child Thalia. It had seemed laughable to Sycorax that such a red, screeching thing should have a name at all, let alone one taken from a muse. "The muse of comedy," Stamos had replied, as though that made it reasonable. "Besides, it's a beautiful name, and she's a beautiful girl."

"Your wits are addled," Sycorax said. But she agreed to the name. She couldn't think of any alternative. And everyone else thought it was a lovely choice.

"I must get back," she said, handing the squirming bundle to the far more expert arms of the wet nurse. Sycorax rose and smoothed invisible dust from the folds of her dress.

Stamos nodded to her absently. His eyes were fastened to his daughter's face, now quiet again and happily chewing her own small fist. Sycorax doubted that he heard her leave the room.

Well, it was she who had pushed him away. It had been nothing to twist his thoughts from her onto their child. *Let him have some happiness,* she told herself. Keeping him at a distance was the best way to protect him.

She went to her room. Not to her chambers. Those were full of servants and companions. No, she went down, by the stone stairs her art had formed, to the underground crypt no one else could enter.

It was cool there, even in midsummer heat. As ever Sycorax shivered, briefly, when the door fell shut behind her. She reached for her fine wool robe and settled it around her shoulders, no longer having to look or even think to do this.

Not that she could see. No light penetrated this room. She moved through the blackness to her worktable. There she held her hand over a wax candle, and a quick blue flame sprang from the wick. It flooded the room with an unusual amount of light. But she did not look at the fire itself. She was very careful to avoid chance visions.

She had trained herself to be blind.

The smooth wooden table was neatly organized. She was systematic in everything. Three walls of the small room were entirely shelved. To her right the shelves contained glass flasks, filled with the tinctures and potions and preserves she needed for her work. They were all stoppered against corruption. On the opposite wall were the objects she required: murderer's hair, hollow stones, small dried animals with their spirits trapped within them. Behind her, on the wall punctured by the door, were the books and scrolls she had gathered and written. Some texts were so ancient that she kept them whole with a constant spell. It was a small thing, no strain.

Before her was the great map. It filled the wall, and on it was drawn the entire known world. At the center was, of course, her own land. With it she could watch any threat brewing against her people and turn it away before it even approached.

The map was her own invention. She had created it five years before, when she was only fifteen years old. Prior to that she had joined her magic with that of the palace wizards to turn aside enemies. That had been a more obvious, dramatic spellcasting, but this was far greater. Her map divinations gave the people of her land the gift of constant, unthreatened peace. She managed all of it here, alone. The other magic-users rarely met with her, and they almost never consulted her. Their arts were all used to provide bountiful harvests, healthy children, and vigorous workers.

They were the sunlit heroes, now. She was a mythical figure, spoken of with fear and whispers. Servants treated her as though she were sacred. Some would no longer say her name. They called her "The Lady."

Sycorax pushed back her resentment and got to work. Her regular regime of watchfulness had faltered. It had been easy to fill her days writing lists and making notes for some future time. She had even gone out into the countryside to gather supplies, which was ridiculous. Servants had done that for her from the time she was twelve.

Wandering around had only made her feel more isolated, anyway. She had no place there, among common people. They needed her to do what only she could do. So she had stopped her foolish roving and returned to her post.

In the corner, where the potions met the map, there was a small hand pump. She used it now, filling the silver basin beneath the nozzle with the earth's deep water. Carefully she brought the basin to the table and placed it in the center, where she could easily glance from it to the map before her.

Flame showed greater variety, but the images were swift and fleeting and gave little context. Water was also constantly changing, but the visions it provided moved more slowly and gave a broader sense of time and place. She gazed into the basin. Her own reflection looked back. Even the rippled surface could not hide her sadness. She looked past it.

To the South she saw internal strife. Kings plotted and moved against each other, with no thoughts to spare for her land. It had been that way for some time. She moved on to the East. Grave threats had come from there in the past, but she and the other wizards had taught them caution. They would not return for at least a generation.

The North was a barbarous place, and their most common enemy. It had wizards of its own, but none to match her. Their threat was like a rheumatic ache: always there, but never overwhelming.

Sycorax turned to the West. These were lands her country traded with, but distance had kept terms civil. She sifted through the visions mechanically, expecting the usual results. Then abruptly she checked herself.

There was a future king whose eyes stared directly back into her own.

She looked up at the map. The vision sped toward its source, a small land of grapes and grain.

And it had something she wanted.

I.v.

Sycorax stood at the wide window, gazing out to the distant sea. That smear of quiet blue she had seen had been the wild road that brought her here. She had used its power to draw Alonso to her, with a useless army at his back and false dreams of glory in his mind. He had answered her call without ever hearing her voice, never realizing that his thoughts of conquest were not really his own.

When he found himself a prisoner in her father's kingdom, his soldiers caught like flies in the amber of her magic, it had been so easy to win him. He had snatched at her offer of help like a drowning man grabs any floating bit of wreckage. She snared him, and together they fled the trap she had set.

She always got what she wanted.

Now she was queen in a foreign land. It should not feel so strange. She was a king's daughter. From her childhood she had commanded servants and walked the corridors of state with confidence. Her only hope was that she hid her bewilderment well. It was not yet clear whom she could trust.

No, that was untrue. It was all too evident that she could trust no one. Even her new husband had become cold, remote. Her belief that they were two trees from the same root was gone. She had given up everything for this land where eyes did not seem to match words. Her decision to betray her home and run away with Alonso had been made carefully, without hesitation. But not without consequences.

And now this new country did not want her. She had used her gifts to master its language. A queen must be able to speak to her people, she had reasoned. She had been wrong. They whispered the word "witch" every time they spoke of her. The servants crossed their fingers behind their backs in her presence. Children were kept away from her. Pregnant women avoided her. She had become a curse.

She would not cling to Alonso. He had used her to win his freedom. The bond they shared was born of his desperation and her cunning. It was not real. She saw that now. But she was too proud to weep at her foolishness. As long as he treated her with dignity, she would find a way to thrive in her new home.

And he would treat her well. He knew her power. No one knew it better. She had wielded dark forces to give him the strength to fight free of her father's enchantments and traps. He had seen her pull power from the moon to shift the tides and send them out to sea. He had lain silently in the boat and watched as she drew the winds around her and sent them flying over the waves, back to his land, back to his throne.

She twisted her hands together, as though wrenching her fingers could tear away the memories she knew were coming next. Because it had not been just a glorious spell of freedom that had set her on this path. She had used her magic to kill Stamos. The thought of him hammered her with fresh condemnation.

But she had to be a widow, free to wed, free to rule. And she had to break all ties with her past, sever all claims upon her father's kingdom. So she had left Thalia. She had abandoned her small daughter. *My heart*, Sycorax had called her. Then she left Thalia for another heart. A false one.

The door opened behind her and she turned, her face expressionless. She still wore the dress of her people: a simple white gown, a band of gold around each arm, her honey-colored hair woven in a braided crown around her head. She knew it irritated her husband, but she could not yet bring herself to wear the heavy dark clothing of his court.

Alonso stood impassively for a moment, his dark eyes impossible to read, his own face a mask of calm. As always there was something about the tilt of his head and the directness of his gaze that made her think of a wild hawk. He was fierce. She had known it from the first moment, seen his strength even in her divinings, even as he kneeled in bloody rags before her father's throne. It was what made her love him.

And he loved me too, she reminded herself. She was sure of it. She remembered how their passion had gripped them both with its sudden force. *He told me that I amazed him*, she thought. *He said that I was his lioness.*

Well, he was the lion. This was a land of fiery men and

shadow-women. And so here he was again, come to school her in the ways of his people. "Cast your eyes down." Was she never to meet the gaze of anyone? "Don't stride across the room." Even her manner of walking offended his court. "A woman must be meek. The queen must be the best of all women." So she, the lioness, was to become the mouse.

She was tired of these lessons, but she listened and nodded. She must try to adapt her ways. *Will there be anything left of me?* she wondered. And then what he was saying next stopped all other thoughts.

"You must not speak in council. It is strange enough that I allow you there at all. It will take them time to grow accustomed just to your presence. When you speak out as you did today, it troubles them. They are not used to hearing the thoughts of women on such matters. They cannot hear what you say, they can only wonder that I let you speak at all. You must share your thoughts only with me, in private."

"But surely we should begin as we mean to go on. They will be used to hearing my thoughts soon enough, as you are."

His gaze shifted, slid away to the window. "It is better my way," he said. "If you cannot be silent you must stay away from council altogether."

That made her silent indeed.

I.vi.

The door shut soundlessly behind Sycorax. She stood against the cool stone of the wall for a moment, making sure that she had not been followed. It was a clear moonlit night. She'd have to take great care not to be seen. She drew the hood of her black cloak closer, clutching it at the neck as she quickly muttered the words of a concealment spell. It would protect her from those who looked down from above. Satisfied, she stole across the small side garden and out the final door in the wall. The guard posted there did not even glance her way as the door opened and shut.

Quickly, she was within the outskirts of the wood, the trees whispering their welcome. She had always been well served by the trees. In a short time she came to the clearing. Here was the magic circle where the moon shone directly upon a large flat white rock. She had seen this place from one of the high towers. Certainly her husband would never agree to her roaming about in the forest. He knew only too well the strength she could find here.

Stone power. That was what she needed right now. The power to withstand her enemies in the court. She must become a fortress.

Because she had many enemies now. It had not taken long for the secrets of her marriage to become common knowledge. And as soon as it was known that Alonso did not love her, that he also found her foreign ways alarming and strange, the dance of the courtiers began. They tried to win his favor by insulting her. He did not protect her. His sense of obligation had diminished. Soon it would be gone altogether. And now that he was surrounded and rooted in his own place of power, he did not fear her as he had.

She stripped off her cloak and knelt on the rock. Wearing only a thin, white gown, her flesh puckered immediately in the chilly night air. She drew the small flint dagger from her belt, intending to lift it to the moon and begin the slow, harsh song of the stone spell. But she paused, then froze.

She had been followed. Sycorax could sense him somewhere in the shadows. Her nostrils flared, testing the wind. There. He was crouched low beneath the fir tree. One of her husband's men, probably a soldier. She knew that he would not be open to bribery.

Her mind raced, but she kept her body still, calm. She must disguise her purpose, make her kneeling here on the ceremonial rock seem innocent. Fortunately, she had not begun the rites. Ideas tumbled through her mind like pebbles in a stream, until one shone clear. She tucked the knife back into her belt, then lowered her face into her hands and began to sob.

It was not hard to cry. She had been holding back tears for so long that they were grateful for a chance to flow. She wept for her child, her father, for her lost land, for the life she would have had, for the life she'd dreamed of, and for the work of her own foolish hand in all her troubles.

It worked. She felt the soldier draw back, hesitate. She sensed his shame. He had followed a woman to catch her committing a crime, and instead he had to witness her loneliness and sorrow. Even so, he did not leave. That annoyed her, for it meant that she would have to go back to her rooms with the rites undone. Who knew when she would get another chance, especially now that her stone had been discovered. But there was no help for it. Though inwardly she seethed, outwardly she kept the ruse of a fragile and broken woman. She wrapped her cloak around herself and stole back to the castle, pausing every now and then to sigh and weep some more. The shadow was behind her the whole way.

Back in her chambers Sycorax paced angrily. She was in danger now, that much was clear. Her husband hoped to free himself of his foreign wife. He needed only to catch her performing her outlawed magic and he would have his reason. The queen could not be a witch.

She clenched the fabric of her skirt in rage. The banning of magic had been a master stroke of his, without a doubt. She had sat beside him, mute and powerless, while he persuaded the council that the use of magic, which had enslaved his own royal person, must be considered a grievous crime. They had agreed readily, their eyes gleaming and victorious in the glances they stole at her from beneath lowered lids. And she had been allowed to do nothing more than vent her fury at him in private, reminding him that it was magic that had saved his royal life, her magic, and that she was the only one who would suffer from their law.

Which, of course, was the reason for the law.

Not that Alonso admitted the truth. He had been sympathetic, of course, but determined. "You have no need for your magic here," he had told her. "Here you need to concern yourself only with matters befitting a royal wife."

She had been silenced then, as she had been so many times before. Alonso meant to take every last shred of power she had, meant to leave her a hollow husk that he could blow away with the breath of a single word. She had been a fool to think that she could control him.

Now he was coming here. She was not surprised. His man must have reported to him, and he had come to satisfy his curiosity, to determine the truth himself. She allowed herself one whispered curse, then sat on her favorite chair. There she leaned back as though she were too weak to support herself. She slowed her breathing and willed herself to look pale.

He was here, beside her, without even knocking. She startled, only some of it feigned.

"I heard you were poorly," he said, his eyes capturing hers.

She pretended confusion. "I am well," she replied, falteringly.

"Hmmph." He was not convinced; she saw that clearly. "I had you followed," he said.

So, it was to be open combat, then. She relished this.

The blood rose in her cheeks. "You did what?" she said.

He waved a hand at her. "You acted your part very well. My man is convinced that you are nothing more than a woman distraught and alone."

"And so I am," she pointed out.

Alonso flapped a hand at her again. "You're as alone as a shark in the sea," he said, "and about as dangerous."

"Dangerous!" she snorted derisively. "How am I dangerous? I have no allies here to defend me, I cannot even speak in public, and now I am forbidden to practice my craft, even privately!"

"Craft! I have seen what your 'craft' is, and what it can do. And don't make claims upon my obligation again," he said, lifting his hand as she opened her mouth to protest. "You have sung that song enough. It was your magic that snared me in the first place."

"Snared you! Poor fellow, what aid could you call upon – other than your army of three thousand men, that is." She turned from him and walked to the window, gripping the sill with both hands, her breathing ragged. He had guessed the truth.

But he paused his attack. She had scored a hit herself, and he had enough grace not to force the point. But that grace only extended so far. He would have his way.

"We must resolve this," he said at last. "I offer you a small estate in Carthage. It has belonged to my family for over a hundred years. It's yours, where you may live out your life in dignity and in the manner you choose. You must only promise me that you will not practice your art against my interests. What do you say to this?"

Banished. To some forgotten place in barren Carthage, the mausoleum of the world. It was fitting, perhaps; a once great city for a once great queen. She gripped the sill of the window even harder, till her fingers were white and the knuckles stood out like jagged stones. Was this the best that her power could do?

"And you?" she asked.

"Me?" His voice was neutral, guarded. He knew what she meant.

"Will you marry again, perhaps make a queen of that pale-faced girl who smiles so much at our table?"

He was silent. It was a direct hit.

"I have a state to run," he said at last. "For its stability, I must have heirs, heirs who are respected as legitimate."

Not the offspring of a foreign enemy, a traitorous queen. Not a witch's spawn.

"I will go," she said. "Make your arrangements."

To his credit, Alonso said nothing as he left.

I.vii.

She was troubled. Her maids had begun to look at her strangely, casting knowing glances at her belly. The secret could not be kept much longer. Sycorax did not like to think what would happen then. She was supposed to leave within the fortnight, as soon as the ship was ready and the rains had stopped.

She stood by the window now, watching the rain, her arms wrapped protectively around her waist. If she had been any other queen, the arrival of a child would have secured her position. This baby would do nothing for her but endanger her life.

She'd been foolish, madly foolish, not to have destroyed it a month ago when she'd first made the discovery. She knew the herbs that would deliver a woman from her trouble. Instead, she had clung to the small life. It was hers. It was all she had. And now it might prove to be the death of her.

Alonso would never tolerate it, not even if it was a girl. There was no way he would allow her to have any claims on his throne and power. Her only hope was to hide the pregnancy until she was safely settled in Carthage. Once she was there she could practice her art and defend both herself and her child.

Sycorax tightened her grip around her waist. Two weeks was not a long time to conceal matters, but her body had already begun to thicken. Her maids would notice any binding and guess the cause. She would have to risk a spell.

She twitched her shoulders, trying to shake away her fears. Alonso had grown sensitive to her magic. He said he could smell it on her.

But it was not really fear of her husband that kept her from her craft. It was the fact that she had to fear him because her powers were weakening. She'd pulled from earth and moon, fire and stone, and she still didn't have the strength to shield herself. For the first time in her life, she was nothing much more than a common woman.

Sycorax twitched her shoulders again. The king never came to see her now. The king. When was the moment when Alonso had stopped being her husband? What had been the final break? Her maids were happy to let her know that he was often in the company of the pale lady. She was a quiet, graceful creature. She'd make a perfect queen. Her children would be welcomed. Joyfully.

Well, there was nothing she could do about that. She turned her thoughts back to the spells she could work. There were only a few that didn't require material elements for the casting. She could put a confusion spell on the maids, make them forget their suspicions about her. But such spells were tricky to control. They might all start blundering about, unable to remember where the clean linen was stored. It would take very little to convince people that she was doing magic. They'd burn her without a qualm.

Or it would have no effect at all. She began to shiver, though she had neither chills nor fever. She was afraid.

"I am afraid."

She said the words aloud. They were ridiculous, preposterous. How could she be afraid of anything, anyone? That she had come to this! Powerless, alone, fearing – *fearing!* – for her very life. The foreign emotion was quickly overwhelmed by a more familiar fury.

She began to break things. A wine glass, a chair. She tore a tapestry hanging on her wall to shreds. She ripped the wedding ring from her finger and threw it into the fire. She commanded the blaze to melt it. The flames rose briefly, then died back to a pale splutter. Her pitiful weakness was never more obvious. She raged and wept and slashed a painting of her husband's grandmother with a shard of broken glass.

Finally she sat down in the middle of the wreckage. She was broken. She might as well be dead.

That would certainly make things easier for the king. She'd be quietly buried, discreetly gone. How triumphant he'd be! The pale lady would be queen, no taint upon her throne, their children.

Sycorax would not let that happen. There was revenge to be had. There was her unborn child to protect.

If magic could not help her, she would have to use the skills of any ordinary woman. Perhaps she could starve herself. She remembered hearing her nurse gossip about a servant who had eaten only one piece of bread every day and concealed her pregnancy for more than seven months.

At that moment a maid entered with a tray of food. She often ate in her room now, avoiding the dining hall and her husband's coldness as much as possible. She could tell from the savory smell that her meal was some sort of venison stew.

The maid stopped and gaped at the destruction of the room. *I am a queen,* she reminded herself. She stood, summoning all her dignity. "Leave the tray on the window seat," she commanded. "I will be taking a walk in the garden after I eat. Have the room tidied before I return."

Her maids had grown scornful, but this one had enough sense to obey. Likely, she thought her fate would be the same as the painting's if she did not. She set the tray down, curtsied, and fled the room.

There was stew, thick and full of meat. And wine. Rich red wine, the one truly fine thing that came from this country. She stared at the bowl. Her stomach rumbled. It seemed like she was always hungry now. It was ridiculous. When she was pregnant with Thalia she hadn't been able to eat a thing for months.

With a girl, pale and drawn. With a boy, healthy and strong. Her ancient nurse's words came back to her. The thought made her laugh: a strange, barking, humorless sound.

She threw the bowl of stew into the fire. It hissed and sizzled, filling the room with foul smoke. She was about to throw the bread into the grate as well, but her grumbling stomach protested.

It was only necessary to slow the baby's growth. Wolfishly she gobbled the bread, then sat and drank the wine. She watched her supper burn and waited for the air to clear.

When her glass was empty she put it down and slipped her arms around her belly once more. She remembered sitting like this when her daughter was growing within her. Then she had been revered, her child wanted, the birth anticipated by everyone. "Thalia," she whispered, "have you cursed me?"

She rose, threw her cloak around her shoulders, and left the room.

I.viii.

They had cut her hair so that it hung around her shoulders in lank, jagged chunks. It looked as though it had been chopped with a scythe. Sycorax was dressed in nothing but a dingy white shift, her feet bare and chapped, her toes curling against the rough wooden planks.

It had not taken them long to discover her secret. She had become sloppy after eating nothing for three days except water, red wine, and a little bread. The maids found the half-burned food. Her ordinary woman's plan was easily understood by the ordinary women around her. The news had spread throughout the palace. She supposed that saved her. Alonso had been quick in sending the doctor. His examination had been short and brutal, conducted while her husband looked on, his eyes blazing. "You thought you could hide this from me," he'd hissed. She'd made no reply.

She had not expected to live. They had charged her with witchcraft and thrown her into prison. They left her there, in the dank, for a week. Finally, the sentence was brought down. She was to be taken by ship to some remote, unchartered place and left there. The judge said she could find mercy at the hands of God and nature.

At first she'd thought that they meant to sail out some distance and then throw her into the sea, but it had been five days now and they still brought her the pathetic bread and water to drink each morning and night. It seemed that Alonso could not bear the title of "baby killer."

That made her laugh, her new dry, empty laugh. How many babies had he and his soldiers killed in all the years he'd warred against other lands? But his own child, however hated, must be shown mercy. She remembered, with infinite irony, how he hoped history would call him, "Alonso the Just."

He had told her that on another sea voyage. How long had it been since they crossed the sea alone together in a small boat, sped by her power, sustained by their love? Less than a year. They had lain together on the bottom of the boat and laughed at the pictures they saw in the clouds. He had played with one of her thick braids, tickling her nose with its feathery tip. The waves had lulled them both. They had been free.

"I should have known it was a fool's happiness," she said aloud. She routinely muttered to herself now. Often she spoke to the shadows of her past. "I deserve to be brought down for what I've done. But I also deserve to destroy him. If I do, then maybe I will be forgiven for betraying my father and my country. Alonso was always my enemy. I'll ruin him." She made it a promise to the small life within her.

There was a cry from on deck. Land had been sighted where none was known to exist. The command was given to sail near, to check for inhabitants. She felt light-headed and lay down on her hard bed, likely the last bed that she would ever know. She waited, time spinning out before her like thread from a spool dropped by a careless child.

It did not take long for the report to come back. A boatload of men had searched the island. It was fair enough, but small, and desolate.

This place, then, was to be her final home. She would die here, and so would her child. Her thoughts of revenge seemed pitiful and desperate. Her husband would have a long, satisfied life. His reign would be legendary. She would become a storybook villain, used to frighten children into obedience. Curses began to flow from her as though they were her mother tongue.

When they came for her, Sycorax fought them like any other caged and cornered beast would. Her wildness gave them permission to be rough with her. She was thrown into the bottom of the boat. Two men actually sat on her to keep her still. They laughed at her and swapped several lewd and boorish comments. When they reached the shore, they called her a hag and flung her onto the rocks. Their only mercies were a small cooking kettle and a blanket they tossed onto the beach with their parting jeers. And so she called down the storm.

As soon as her body had touched the land, she found her power again. It was shaky, its flow only a trickle after so many months of disuse. But it was there, singing in her veins, intoxicating her. The wind tore the ship to shreds and the waves swallowed the boat whole. Now it was her turn to laugh, while the sailors could only scream. She danced on the rocks as the last of them disappeared. Mermaids bobbed in the waves, pulling the lost men down.

The tempest died as quickly as it had begun. She was alone, and now she had nothing to curse but her own stupidity. She should never have let her emotions rule her craft. There had been a ship at her disposal, and she sank it. She could have destroyed only the sailors and then gone to Carthage, to the estate awaiting her rule. She could have sailed back to her husband and cursed his land.

She could have gone home.

The weight of her punishment came down on her again. She could never go home. There was penance to be paid before she could win back her freedom, before she could wreak her revenge.

She left the beach and went inland, like an animal, looking for shelter. After a short search she found a cave, empty of wildlife. For now it would do. Doggedly she gathered wood, refusing to think of her past life, her royal life. The fire warmed her, and the mushrooms that she found under some trees stilled the gnarling pain in her belly. Sycorax went back to the trees, this time breaking off fir boughs and dragging them back to the cave for a bed. They were fragrant and surprisingly soft. She slept.

When she awoke it was deep night. She rose and left her cave. The moon shone brightly. The air was warm, gentle. She felt and relished the trusting fertile power of the land. The soft breeze lifted her mood. This could be as much a time of healing as it was of atonement. Sycorax searched the ground until she found what she sought. Flint, bleached white in the moonlight. She found another stone and began to chip away. This, at any rate, was familiar. It was in just such a manner that she had fashioned her other knife, the one she had never used.

She paused. Who would find it beneath the corner flagstone of her sleeping-chamber floor? Would it be some distant royal child, casting about for something to do? Would he cut himself on the blade, have it taken from him by a scolding nurse?

She bent her head again. It would not be her child who found it.

I.ix.

Caliban was crying again. She had been gone too long this morning. The fish seemed to be growing more clever and were evading her traps. But she had won in the end, bringing home three fine trout. She slipped into the cave and stirred up the coals of the cooking fire. She hung the fish over the glowing heat to cook, then went to the bough bed and lifted up her small son.

He nuzzled against her, drinking greedily. His rusty hair stood up in tufts all over his head. His birthmarks were an angry dark purple, thanks to his wailing. She stroked his head and smiled at him. "My wild child," she crooned.

Caliban was ugly. She knew it. His head was so strangely proportioned. She had hoped his narrow forehead and his broad jaw were simply the result of his difficult birth, that they would smooth themselves into something resembling her own. But time had not changed his features. He was squat and thick and speckled, with short limbs that promised strength without grace.

None of that mattered. He was hers.

The cave was filled with the sounds of the food cooking, the child eating, her own soothing song. This was one of the happy times of her day, when the fight for survival paused and she could sit for a moment with her child. She could forget, for a short time, the life she'd lost. The anger would ease, and she could let herself drift free of memory.

When the child finished his meal reality pressed back in upon her. She could not go on like this, scrabbling about from day to day. The first few months on the island had passed in a blur of exhaustion and sickness. She managed to make the cave habitable, but most days she could not stand its gloom. So she had fashioned herself a nesting place on a bluff overlooking the ocean. No ship came near enough to be snared by her magic. Her pregnancy weakened her, the baby drawing from her bones when she did not find food. She grew to hate the smell and taste of fish.

It had been hot and dry when Caliban was born. She had retreated to the cave, its dark coolness suddenly a refuge. She'd stored up water and food for the time of his birth, had gathered all the herbs she could that would speed his coming. When at last her waters broke she was ready. She'd expected an easy delivery. He was her second child, and her daughter had been born without trouble. But her pains stretched on endlessly through the day and into the night. She had no midwives to help her. There was no one to rub her back or bring her water. She scrabbled about on the dirt floor, cursing Alonso. But she could not curse his blood, for it also flowed in the veins of her son.

She was bruised and torn by the time he slid free of her. She managed to catch him and lay him on a soft heap of cloth, the remnants of her clothing. He lay still and did not breathe. She held him upside down and thumped his back. She remembered women saying midwives did that when the child was born blue and silent. He choked and gasped and finally screamed. She'd held him to her breast until he grew quiet. There was no wet nurse for him. They slept beside each other on the floor that night, her blood pooling on the dirt. Somehow, they both lived. She would not die. Caliban would not die. She promised him, when she first brought him out into the sunlight, that she would bring him back to his kingdom. "You are royal," she said to him. "You are beloved of the gods."

Now that her strength was back she could once more turn her mind to escape and revenge. There was power here, great power. Magic grew on the island as commonly as mushrooms after a rain. But she could not harness it. It slipped free of every attempt to take it and use it for her own ends.

There were also magical beings everywhere, but after an initial passing curiosity, they ignored her. She knew why. The island was littered with the bleached skeletons of drowned sailors washed ashore, or of shipwrecked men who had lived for a time, then been taken by disease or starvation. The island expected the same fate for her.

She rose and lifted Caliban into a sling she wore draped over her shoulder and across her chest. It was made from the thin blanket she had been left with. She did not like to think what she would do when it wore away. There were times, in the chill loneliness of night, when she would lie and stroke the rough wool, remembering the rich, soft, sweetly scented bed of her home. When Caliban nuzzled her in the small morning hours, she'd think of Thalia asleep in a silken cradle, a wet nurse ensuring that Sycorax's own royal slumber would not be broken. She wondered if her father would be pleased to know her fate. She thought of his proud, stern face, how it had beamed at her with satisfaction when she lied to him about the spells she had cast. He never questioned her.

She shook her head, trying to free her mind of the guilt that threatened to smother her as completely as her rage. She went out into the sunlight, Caliban crowing with pleasure at the chance to be out in the clean island air, away from the smoky murk. She was determined that today she would root out the source of the island's power.

She wandered among the trees, listening to their secret language of whispers and light. She had done this every day since her arrival here, except for the week of Caliban's birth. But the trees were strangely distant, as though they knew her goal and wished to thwart her, to keep the power for themselves.

It was the same thought she'd had hundreds of times before, but now it broke across her mind like a wave against the rocks. That was just what they were, these trees: jealous guardians of power. She lay her palms against a pine and pulled. The power was not there, but the surprised tree cried out and showed her where to look. She turned and strode, with Caliban chirping on her hip, to the summit of the island.

It seemed so obvious, when she arrived, that the wild apple

tree was what she had been looking for. It spread its boughs wide, hard little fruit littering the ground beneath it. It was food and shelter for many creatures. It was the life of the island.

She placed her hands against its trunk, felt it sing with power and fear. The tree had known she would claim it, had hoped that she would die before she could. "I did not die," she said to it, grinding her teeth spitefully.

The night of the full moon was nine days away. She had plenty of time to ready herself for the rites. She turned and went back to the cave, deafening herself to the pleas she heard and felt all around. In nine days she would tear down the tree and bind its power for her own use. Then…well, then she would have the means to win her freedom.

She sang as she walked.

I.x.

The moon was full, golden, swollen with power, and at the height of its strength. Caliban was sleeping peacefully when she left. She had woven a small charm so that he would not awake. The trees seemed to catch at her with their branches, trying to stop her. She brushed them away. Her need was greater than that of any tree. She could not be stopped.

The apple tree seemed to glow in the watery light of the moon. She stood for a moment and observed it, admiring it. It was kin to her, somehow. And soon it would belong to her.

Sycorax strode across the clearing, the knife gripped firmly in her right hand. All the great spells required blood for the casting. She took comfort that this spell would not require her to bleed alone.

Silver light made everything stark. She drove the blade into the tree, past its thick skin and into the quick. Normally stone would not be equal to the task, but her words and the moon strengthened the knife. Resolutely, she pushed it down, carving the symbol of power deep into the tree's heart. Sap oozed from the cut. Steadily she carved, until the sign was complete. She pulled the knife free.

Her hand clenched, involuntarily. Sycorax forced it open and glared at it, as though it were a belligerent child that needed to be disciplined. In the colorless light she stared at her palm, her fate mapped in its creases.

Panic rose in her throat, but she pushed it back. She would cut a new line, write a new fate in the flesh of her hand.

The thought of Caliban steadied her. She would do anything to win him back his rightful place. He would not live here, like some lost wolf-child.

She slit her palm, driving deep into the muscle. Then she placed her wound against the tree's, blood to blood. The knife fell from her other hand and shattered. That was of no importance. It was no longer needed. She began to chant the words of the spell. Her voice was rough, hoarse. It was hard to think, harder still to speak, through the red mist of pain. Waves of nausea battered her. Grimly she fought on. She would not fail.

The magic of the tree's veins flowed into her own. Her hair began to crackle as though it was burning, but she felt herself growing cold. In spite of her shivering, she did not move her hand, she did not let the song falter. It was a battle for control she was waging, and she was determined to win. But the roots of the tree ran into the heart of the island, and its power was more than she'd ever imagined. Everything that lived and breathed and grew and died upon the island was attached to the tree. All its life surged in rebellion against her.

The owls were the first to attack. She felt them coming and leaned into the tree to protect her face from their buffeting wings and razor claws. They tore at her hair, her back, and shoulders. She beat them off with the magic of the tree, but the power was divided. They came on again. She tucked her head under her arm. Her voice was only a whisper now, but she did not stop the spell.

It was when she sensed the vipers coming that her heart nearly failed. Sycorax had never lost her childhood fear of snakes. The tree knew this, and brought them on more swiftly.

She would lose, and die. Caliban would also die, alone, never waking from his magical sleep. It was not fair that an innocent child should have to pay such a high price for her failure.

Fury came to her aid. It blasted every fear from her mind. The bitter gall of her guilt and suffering and humiliation flooded her. She would not lose her son. In a blaze of hatred she ripped the power from the island's very roots.

The tree burned, engulfed in icy flames that ate their own heat. She remained unharmed. The moonfire continued to rage, forcing back the owls and the serpents. The power of the tree was drawn inward, until at last the fire died and she was left holding a blackened staff. It didn't look like much of a royal scepter, but it was the channel her magic now flowed through.

Sycorax staggered back toward the cave, leaning on the staff for support. Her new power threatened to overwhelm her. She was aware of every heartbeat, every stone-crack on the island. And all of it waited, breath suspended, to see what life would be like, now that it was in thrall to the island queen.

Somehow she made it home. Sycorax collapsed on the bough bed, drawing Caliban to her. Once the staff was out of her grasp, the call of the island grew fainter. She slept.

As soon as she awoke the island cacophony was there again. She had not bargained on this, on having the mind of every creature hammer at her own thoughts. She would have to find a way to make them quiet, or she would go mad.

Caliban was still sleeping. He would not wake until she willed it. Sycorax brushed her guilt away. Let him sleep a little longer. Now she had power to test. With the staff in her hand, she left the cave.

She felt her way through all the small lives on the island, peering at each one and gauging its usefulness before moving on to the next. At last she made a great discovery. A smile curled her lips.

"Come," she said.

A creature of air and fire appeared before her. "Ariel," she said, pulling his name from him.

"Yes," he replied.

"You are my servant now," she said. It was unnecessary, but she enjoyed hearing the words come from her mouth.

"Yes," he said again. It seemed to her that his fire burned lower, and grew pale. Well and good. He should know better than to test her authority.

"Bring me food," she ordered. "Bread, and fruit, and properly cooked meat; lamb, I think. And wine, rich red wine. Have it here within the hour."

"Yes," he said.

"And a crown," she said. "A golden one, with jewels. I don't care where you get it from." She smiled and waved her hand to dismiss him.

In an instant he was gone. She did a little dance of joy on the shore.

I.xi.

Wherever Sycorax walked a pall of silence fell, as though every-thing were holding its breath, waiting for her to pass by. She was poison, stench, plague, and swarm to the island. She was the heart of every tempest. Her power, born of anger and won by hatred, could find no peace in its expression. The creatures of the island despised her. The mermaids howled abuses at her from the safety of the sea, always staying beyond the reach of her control. Once, Sycorax had picked up a rock, marveling at its perfect shape, and knew at once that it longed to crush her. How could a stone hold such hate?

But she could not leave. She had fused her very soul to this island. She had planned to drain it of its strength and use its force to wreak a glorious revenge. Instead, she had bound her-self to it. If she left she would die, and what would happen to Caliban then? In seeking to win her freedom, she had built herself a cage.

Disappointed and thwarted hopes made a bitter brew to swallow, and she had to drink it every day. It made her savage and cruel. She could not tame herself; she did not remember how to feel mercy. Only this morning she had imprisoned Ariel in a pine tree. He had not been as swift on an errand as she desired. His groans and howls would wring pity from the stoniest heart. But Sycorax felt nothing but blind rage. It drove all other thoughts from her mind. She knew that she would not let Ariel out, no matter how much she suffered from the loss of his service. She scorned her own stupidity, but could not stop herself. It was as if her mind and her will had been cleaved apart, never to be rejoined. Every day Sycorax died a little more, and there was only a mad monster left to rule this small world.

She flung curses at the sea, sending out another storm to toss a ship ashore. Sycorax filled her days by combing the shore for lost treasures caught by the waves. Her cave was now hung with rich fabrics, though all of them were water-stained and moldering. She ate off fine china once more. Thin, delicate plates, every one of which was cracked or chipped. The elegant clothes she scavenged and wore were ill-fitting and torn. At least the gold she found still shone. It was a comfort to her. She hoarded it, burying it safe in a deep hole. "I've become a dragon," she would say to herself, and then she'd look down at her hands, expecting to see scales and claws in their place. The gold had grown to a considerable pile. One day it would be Caliban's, his birthright. He was a king's son, after all.

The only gentle moments for her now were those with her small son, speaking with him in the language of her home. She would not talk to him in his father's tongue. It was foolish of her. If Caliban was to be his father's heir, he must be able to speak with his people. But the syllables twisted in her mouth and refused to fall from her lips. The words choked her, just as her husband's land had choked her power.

She could not even tell Caliban the truth of his parentage. Instead, she had spun him a story to please them both, that he was the child of a god. Setebos, was the name she gave him, this glorious father who lived in the sky and looked down upon them.

"I want him," Caliban would say.

"Gods always leave their earthly children," she told him. "They have heavenly matters to tend to. They leave their small mortal sons to grow strong and brave, to be heroes."

She told him, in whispers, that he was like Heracles, like Perseus.

He stared at her with his wide pale eyes, understanding very little but sensing the wonder in what she said. He would run along the shore pointing at the sun, crying out, "Tetebof! Tetebof!" She would laugh, then. She would feel nearly happy. "Wild boy," she would call him. He'd grin at her, his thick fleshy lips stretching to split his face, his birthmarks purple in the bright light of day. "Catch me a fish," she'd say.

And he would. He could catch anything. He was clever and swift. He was fearless, throwing himself into the waves, leaping across rocks, climbing up cliff faces to steal bird's eggs, to fetch her flowers.

The smile fell from her face. He was not really fearless. Not anymore. He had begun to grow afraid of her when her anger was strongest. His little eyes stared up at her when she raged about the cave. He would sit on their bed like an animal watching a predator, silent and still. On nights when the moon was full he would hide himself away in another smaller cave. She knew where he was, of course. She knew, all the time, where everything was on the island. But she let him feel safe.

She only hoped that he was safe.

The thought made her fall to the ground. She lay there, her knees pulled up to her chest, her hands clutching her ankles. This was something she had discovered by accident several months ago. When she rolled herself up the power looped through her, needing no other target to vent itself upon. It left her bent and weakened, but it protected everything else.

Sycorax knew that someday she would not unbend, that she would die this way, twisted in on herself. It was the only true kindness she had left.

A raven flapped toward her and thumped down on a rock. It croaked and bobbed its head. She had loved these birds, once. In her own country they were revered. They were prophetic and wise. When she was twelve, she'd had one as a pet. Vrok, she'd named it. She fed it bits of meat, and it preened its feathers from its perch on her shoulder. She cried for three days when it left in the spring, seeking a mate.

But this was an island bird. It would never rub its bill playfully against her cheek as Vrok had done. Even in the midst of her pain she could feel its curious eyes upon her. It wondered if she was dead. It hoped she was. She'd make a delightful feast for him and his brothers. She let go of her legs and jumped to her feet, wielding the staff before her. The black bird squawked and tried to lift itself to safety. It was too slow. Lightening shot from the staff and destroyed it, leaving nothing but a stain of ash on the rocks.

Sycorax felt momentary triumph, then contempt. She had killed a bird. A cat could do so much. She made her way back to the cave.

Act Two

Sulfur Sun,
Mercury Moon

II.i.

His mother was lying on the bed when he returned from fishing, twisted in on herself. The staff had fallen from the bed and lay on the ground. Caliban knew better than to bother her when she was like that. He crept about quietly, making his food for the day. But she began to whimper, in the manner of all small, sick things, which she'd never done before. "Never show pain, Caliban," she always said. "Never let anyone think that you're weak." Her mewling cries frightened him, but he did not run away like he usually did when she scared him. Instead, he sat down beside her and ·stroked her hair, kicking the staff away as he did so.

He didn't like it. "Mean stick," he called it. But not in front of his mother. Once he'd asked her why she didn't throw it into the waves, throw it where it couldn't hurt her anymore. "I can't," she said. And then she laughed in such a horrible way, for such a long time. It was worse than crying, that laughter. He never spoke about the mean stick again.

His patting didn't help her. He felt her skin beneath his hand, but he couldn't seem to touch her. She was leaving him. He tried to sing her the songs she once sang to him. Only he couldn't remember all the words, and his voice was rough, not smooth and gentle like hers could be. If his voice was sweeter, maybe he could have saved her. But she did not want to be saved.

He knew the instant she died. She'd been quiet for a while, so it wasn't her silence that told him. She was there with him one moment, and gone the next. Her body did not droop. He stayed beside her, uncertain what to do. He wondered if she'd come back. She was so powerful. He could not imagine her dead the way fish were dead. He wondered if he should eat her. He did not want to. He was not a crow.

Finally she grew hard and stiff, like wood. Caliban did not like to see her face. Her eyes were empty. He dragged her body out into the open, down to the shore, hoping she would not snap like kindling. He was strong. She always told him he was strong. He knew that she wouldn't want to be left there, in the dark. She never liked the cave, not the way he did. She called it shelter. He called it home.

He watched from his rock as the tide came up and the waves gently slipped around her. Soon they pulled her out and carried her away. It had grown gray and cold, but Caliban did not leave. He stayed until he could no longer see the dark ring of withered flesh that was all the magic had left of his mother. Rain began to fall. He supposed that Setebos was hiding his face now. He must be sad, too.

But no matter how long Caliban sat with his arms wrapped

around his chest, the aching would not go away. His throat was tight and air didn't seem to fit into his lungs any more. He gasped a bit, like a fish floundering out of water. He stood on the rock and called to his mother. "Come back!" he said. "Come back! You've gone too far!"

But she didn't come back. He knew she wouldn't. And he didn't know what to do with himself. He was used to spending his days alone, but she'd always been somewhere nearby. He'd see her on the beach, dancing and yelling. Or he'd find her in the woods, arguing with some unlucky tree. She'd wake him up at night, when she came in after one of her moonlit walks, to give his back a quick rub before lying down beside him to sleep. Now she was gone, and his island suddenly felt very big. He felt hollow inside.

After a while he left and went back home, where he sat and ate the fish stew he had made earlier. He would only eat the food that came from the island. He had never liked the magical food his mother had her servants bring them. She would smile as she ate it. It made her happy. She'd tell stories of life in her royal court. It was her pretending, he guessed, just as he would pretend to be a shark when he splashed in the shallows. Caliban couldn't understand why she liked her imaginary place so much. She never did anything there but eat and work magic, just like she did here. And it was full of odd and useless people. "They respected me!" she would say. "They feared me." Then he knew it was time to leave. She always got angry after the stories.

It had never nourished her, the magical food. He had watched her grow frail and thin, refusing to eat the good island food he made. "You must," he had said. She had smiled, and ruffled his hair. She had not wanted to live.

Caliban knew why. It lay there, in the corner. The mean stick. It had begun calling to him. It wanted a master.

He looked down at the staff. He knew that it held the island's life. It had held his own. Now it was looking for someone to wield it. "You are the island king," it said. That was one of his mother's pretend words. King and queen. She always said them together. "Setebos is king," he told the mean stick. "He doesn't need you." The mean stick tried to catch him, but he was free of it, freed by his mother's death. He would not be caught by it as she had been. He would not die twisted into a hoop.

At first he tried tossing it into the sea. But his mother was right; it would not float away. No matter how hard and how far he flung it, it would not follow his mother out into the deeps. Time after time it washed up again on the shore. Its voice bothered him. It bothered all the creatures. Birds began to flap about aimlessly in disordered flocks. Pigeons flew with ravens, seagulls swooped by with starlings.

He could burn it in his fire, cook his supper over its coals. But the very idea seemed to make the island shudder. Finally he brought it back into the cave. He scraped together the earth of the floor and buried it, in the corner of the cave. Then he brought in rocks to cover the small mound. Its call was muffled, now. He could ignore it. He would forget it.

He ran out into the falling rain when his task was done.

II.ii.

Caliban had been alone for many years. His language was all but gone. "Fire," he would say, holding his hands up to the heat. "Fish. Water. Cave. Setebos." He would turn his words over in his mind, like stones in a stream, polishing them, keeping them bright and alive.

And now he could share them again. He watched, shaking with fear and hope, with wanting, as a man pulled a small boat onto the shore and then, amazingly, lifted out a sleeping child.

The man stumbled. He was tired, he needed help. Caliban crept from his cover of the trees. He approached slowly, his hands empty, to keep the man from fearing him the way the wild creatures often did.

Even so the man stepped back, alarmed. He was tall, his graying beard long, his hair too. His dark robes were weathered, and his face was newly reddened and peeling from exposure to the sun. Caliban guessed he'd been adrift at sea for several days.

The child in his arms stirred and whimpered. The man spoke to it, his words quick and lilting, none of them familiar to Caliban. They made him feel suddenly ashamed, those slippery, lightning words, as though he were only a beast and not the son of a god.

Then the child lifted its head, and Caliban gasped in wonder. It had golden hair that spilled over its shoulders, gleaming in the sunlight. It must be a god-child too, this beautiful creature. The man spoke again, to him this time, his voice rich and deep. Now Caliban could sense his power. Perhaps he was a god. Perhaps he was even Setebos, come again in the form of a man.

Caliban fell to his knees. He tried to speak, to tell the god that he would serve him, help him, here on the island. But the words strangled in his throat and only a guttural croak came out. He blushed with humiliation, hanging his head lower. This was not how he meant to greet his father.

But then the god put a hand on his shoulder, and the words that he spoke were gentle. Caliban felt such a sudden rush of relief and happiness that he laughed and leapt eagerly to his feet. "Home," he said, gesturing toward the cave. "Home," he repeated, seeing the man's confusion. Strange that Setebos did not understand his mother's language any longer, but perhaps he was not saying the words properly anymore. Instead, he pretended to be eating. That, the man understood.

Carefully, still carrying the golden child, he followed Caliban. He stumbled even more as he carried her over the rocks. It must be hard to walk like a man when he was used to living in the sky,

Caliban thought. Caliban walked slowly, so that the god could be sure of his footing.

The child did not want to go into the cave. It clung to the god's robes and cried, burying its face in his chest. Caliban stirred the stew cooking in the kettle, its rich, savory smell filling the cave. That made the child lift its head. It must be hungry after being at sea.

They ate almost everything in the kettle, the two of them. Caliban kept back only a small portion for himself, just enough to ease the rumblings in his belly. When they'd finished eating the child began to explore the cave, until the god called her back with a few sharp words. He did not look comfortable here, in the smoky darkness. Caliban remembered the homes that his mother described, great structures built of wood and stone that sheltered her from the weather and still let in the light. The god must be used to homes like that when he came to be in flesh. Caliban would build him one here, on the island. He even knew where he would do it.

For Caliban the next few days flew by in a flurry of wonder. He began to build the house and saw that the god was pleased. He taught Caliban his god-words for things, pointing to everything and speaking slowly, waiting for Caliban to repeat it. The child, a girl-child named Miranda, began to teach him too. She soon lost her fear of him and followed him about, pointing to things and then laughing when he tried to imitate her speech. He did not like the laughing. He stopped saying the words to her. The god noticed this and spoke to her sharply again. She became kinder, telling him the words and not laughing anymore.

He worked hard, building the house as the god instructed him. Within a week the roof was on and he'd made beds for each of them. They brought their blankets from the boat and seemed pleased with their new home. Caliban slept on the floor. He liked to be ready to serve the god and his child. He made their fires and brought them food. He carved the girl small animals out of wood. He made her a dolphin and a rabbit. "Make me a dolly," she said. But he didn't know what that meant. "A little child," she explained. "Like me." She pointed to herself, and he understood. She loved the dolly he made her. She was happy.

But the god would walk the shore at times, his face as stormy as the sea. He felt the magic of the island and could not harness it. Caliban knew this, could feel the frustration of his power. He worried about it, shuffling his fear and concern with the desire to please. Finally, he decided that a god, such as the man surely was, would not be tainted by the power.

He went into his cave while the god and the child were sleeping in their new house. Outside it was sunny and warm, and the quiet day had lulled them. But the cave was as cool as ever. It felt odd at first. Something was wrong. Perhaps the cave was cross with him for leaving it. "I have to look after the god," he explained. There was no answer. Well, the cave never talked. Not really. Only the corner. He felt himself shiver. He should make a fire here. That would make the cave happy again. But no, he had come for another reason. Resolutely, he walked to the back corner and knelt by the mound of earth. Its voice was thin, but it could sense him nearby. It guessed his purpose.

"Take me up, I'm yours, I'm yours," it insisted.

It grew more excited as he began to dig. But he would not listen to it. He did not want it, but perhaps the god did. And the god would know what to do with it.

And so he brought Prospero the staff.

II.iii.

Caliban liked the way Miranda always tried to follow him everywhere. He called birds from the sky for her. She clapped her hands and had to stifle yelps of excitement when he did that. Sometimes he folded a leaf into a small boat for her to send down the fishstream, which they then chased together along the bank. Once he carved each of them a whistle from a green bough, and they tried to play music.

But her father did not like her to wander off with him. Whatever they were doing together was interrupted by his stern voice calling, "Miranda! Time to attend to your studies!" Then she turned quiet and went back to the hut. Caliban returned to cutting firewood, or mending clothes, or fishing for supper, or cooking, or some other necessary task. But he felt lonely after Miranda and her laughter had left him. He wished they could play more often.

The spirits of the island had started to tease him now.

Prospero had freed his mother's servant, Ariel, from the pine tree where she had trapped him. Ariel never seemed to pass up an opportunity to make Caliban miserable. "Look at the island king!" he would jeer as Caliban struggled with a load of wood. Then Ariel would fly down and tug on his ears and pull his hair. Caliban would have to drop the logs to swat him away. Sometimes he did that, and they mashed his toes painfully. Most of the time he just endured the torment, gritting his teeth. "Mudman," Ariel would snarl, and then wisp away to tell Prospero that Caliban was napping in the woods.

Prospero always believed the spirit's lies.

Caliban shifted uncomfortably, frowning. He now knew Prospero was not a god. A god would not be so blind. A god would not fart and snore and belch like Prospero did, when he thought no one could hear him. A god would know that Caliban was a god's son, and should not always be the one to hunt for mushrooms and dig the latrine and fetch heavy wooden pails full of water for the washing.

Prospero had wanted a wizard's cape for himself, a cape made from cormorant feathers. Caliban had caught the birds and skinned them. Then he cured the skins so they stayed soft and supple, and finally he sewed the cape. When it was done Prospero had taken it from Caliban and thrown it around his shoulders. "Good work, Caliban," he had said.

But those words didn't warm Caliban the way they used to. Prospero had refused to eat the meat, saying it was unclean. That had horrified Caliban. He had tried to eat it all himself, but he could not do it. Some of the meat went bad. Caliban put it out for the crows to finish.

A god would not be so wasteful.

Caliban pulled the fish trap from the small pool. There were three fat trout inside it. He thanked each of them for being his meal, then he struck them quickly against a rock. It was the same rock he always used for the quick death. He called it the "mercy stone." A small red smear appeared on it, as it had countless times. The rain would wash it away.

But now Caliban stared at the stain. How many creatures had he killed for Prospero? The three fish lay in his lap, cradled. They would have been plenty for himself, but he needed to catch at least three more to feed Prospero and Miranda as well. Caliban and the island gave Prospero everything he needed, and none of it was ever enough.

Caliban had heard him talking to Miranda. He said the island was a land fit for savages. He said the fine hut that Caliban had built in worship was a hovel. He swore that he would choke to death on fish stew.

Swiftly Caliban stood. His vision blurred with hot, angry tears. He clutched the dead fish to his chest. "I thank you for your meat," he said, again and again. He walked without planning his direction, but when he finally came to the cave he knew this was the destination he intended.

The boughs that covered the entrance were dead and dry. He pushed them aside and crept in.

The damp, warm darkness wrapped around him. He stood there for a minute, letting the feeling of home comfort him. Then his memory moved him to the old fire pit. In an instant he was kneeling beside it. There was some kindling, ready and waiting for him. He pulled the flint and steel from his pocket and struck it. The spark flashed and caught. Caliban had a gift with fire.

The wood he'd left in here was well-aged and burned brightly. In no time Caliban's fish were sizzling over the flames. He ate them off the roasting stick, letting the oil smear across his chin. He had no one to impress here, in his own home.

Afterwards, he lay down on the old bough bed and fell asleep. His dreams were odd and unsettling. He found himself wandering through a large, empty stone palace, like the kind his mother used to describe. He wasn't looking for her, though. He didn't know what he was looking for, but he knew he had to find it. Everything shifted around. He walked from the corridor through a door to a room, then found himself back in the corridor. He couldn't reach the stairs he saw at the end of the passageway, no matter how determinedly he walked toward them. And the ceiling kept getting lower, until his hair brushed against it even when he stooped.

He woke up. A compulsion dragged him out of the cave, even though he balked. He did not want to leave, but he had no choice.

It was Prospero's doing. The wizard had summoned him, the way he called his spirit servants. Caliban champed and raged and pulled against his own steps, but he could not stop.

Prospero looked thunderous when Caliban arrived at the hut. "Where have you been?" he bellowed. "It's long past supper! Where are the fish you were sent to catch?"

"I ate them," Caliban growled in response. His heart felt as though it were a smoldering coal in his chest. "If you're hungry, make yourself some food."

Prospero was speechless, but only for an instant. "Insolent wretch!" he screamed. "I have trained you in speech and raised you from beasthood. Is this how you answer me?"

"This is my island!" Caliban yelled back. Spit flew from his lips, but he did not care. "This is my home! Why should I serve you?"

Prospero lowered the staff toward him. "You will do as I say, Caliban."

Pain coursed through his body. He fell to the ground, thrashing like a landed fish as the teeth of agony bit into every nerve of his body. All thoughts fled his mind, except for the one shining hope that the pain would end. It did.

"You will do as I tell you, Caliban. This is my island."

And so Caliban went from servant to slave.

II.iv.

His back had been crippled with pain for the last three days. Prospero promised it would not improve for another four. Caliban didn't care. His prank had been worth it.

He'd put toadstools in their stew. Not the deadly kind. If Miranda didn't share her father's food he would have used those. But she did, so he just taught them both a lesson. They were too stupid to notice. They didn't know anything, for all their fine words and books. They'd lived on his island for ten years now, and they still didn't know what was good to eat.

He remembered their writhing and retching and laughed, even though it made him wince with pain. "You'll suffer too," he vowed to the empty air. And he meant it.

Slowly, breathing carefully after each wrenching step, he made his way to the beach by his cave. There he stripped off his clothes, which caused him to weep and shudder. But he did not stop. Soon he was naked, and he crawled into the sea.

The water was cold, but he didn't care. He pushed himself further from the shore, and each stroke eased the pain. The water loosened the bonds of Prospero's spell. Caliban flipped onto his back and floated, blissfully free of torment. He stared up at the white clouds drifting in their own airy sea. "I'm as free as a cloud," he said. "I can just waft away."

"Or you could come with me," a sly, hissing voice said beside him. He startled, spluttering on a mouthful of brine. Then he saw who had spoken and he grinned. "Hello, Pisces," he said to the mermaid, dredging up his old childhood name for her. "Do you want to drag me to your seabed?"

Peisinoe smiled back at him, her green eyes full of wicked light. She had always been the one he liked best. She used to come to the shore and tell him stories when he was a child and lived here alone. He had spoken to her in jest, but suddenly, here in the waves, he found himself afraid of her. Her hair was slicked against her skull. When it was dry it looked emerald in the sunlight, but now it was nearly black. From this close distance her yellow-green skin looked sickly. "I might take you, Caliban, such a man you've become." She stroked his face with her wet webbed fingers. He could feel the thin frill on her tail fin tickling his feet, then his calves, then knees. A strange heat coursed through him. His ears rang a distant chime and his mind blurred. "Stop that," he said. He pushed away from her and treaded water.

She laughed at him. "Oh, you are a new man indeed, Caliban. You'd better leave the sea and not come back, or I will take you down to lie with me beneath the waves."

Confusion choked him. He turned and swam back to the

shore. Prospero's prison of agony wracked his spine as he pulled himself up on the stony beach. He looked back at the mermaid. Peisinoe met his gaze, then dove under, giving the surface of the water a warning slap with her tail before she disappeared.

Caliban hugged his knees to his chest. Tears of miserable rage poured over his face. He wanted to retreat to his cave, but Prospero wouldn't let him go there anymore.

Soon he would have to gather firewood and pull up the fish trap. Prospero never let him rest. "We must all do what God intended us to do," he would say. "Some of us must labor in muscle, and others of us in the mind." And then he would send Caliban away to sweat and toil, while he sat and brooded over the same dusty pages.

"That windbag doesn't know anything about work," Caliban muttered now. He kicked at the stones by his toes. His back twisted into a new spasm, making him gasp. "I hate him," he whispered.

"Here you are, bad broody," said Miranda. She picked her way gingerly across the stones, as though she was not accustomed to walking on them. In her hands she carried the wooden cup he'd made for her. Caliban's glower increased.

"What do you want?" he growled. He wanted to be alone with his hatred. Miranda was too kind. She would spoil his anger.

She smiled at him. "I've come to make peace," she said. She handed him the cup. "Drink this. It will make you feel better."

He sniffed it suspiciously. It smelled like sunshine and sage. He hesitated.

"It isn't poisonous," she said. "I've convinced my father to forgive you for the toadstools. He agrees that he has been harsh with you lately. You've been punished enough. We're sure you've learned your lesson." She smiled encouragingly, so pleased with her speech.

He drank the potion in one long swallow. The pains in his spine fell away. He felt new vigor and health and strength.

And rage.

"I'm going to build a boat and sail away from here," he said. "You can come with me if you want, but I'm leaving the old man to rot here on his own."

Miranda stepped back from him, appalled. "How can you say such a thing, Caliban? And after my father brewed this potion for you, too!"

"To heal me from the pain he gave me!" Caliban yelled.

Miranda flushed red. "You made us ill, Caliban. You might have killed us!" Her eyes opened wide with horror at the thought.

"If I wanted you dead, you'd be dead," he snarled. "I just wanted to teach both of you a lesson."

"Teach us a lesson; I like that!" Her cheeks flamed redder. "What lesson could you possibly teach us, Caliban? You're a brute. That's what father says, and he's right!" She snatched up the cup and turned on her heel.

Searing white rage flooded him. He leapt forward and grabbed her arms, flinging her back around to face him. She stared up at him, outraged and terrified.

It was the mermaid who had put the thought in his head,

he told himself afterward. And that was true, though it was no excuse. Prospero came over the ridge to find him pushing Miranda to the ground, covering her with his own weight. A bolt of sizzling magic struck him, and he lost consciousness.

When Caliban woke he found himself bound to a rock by chains.

II.v.

Caliban stood on the forward deck of the ship, staring at the smudge of land in the distance. The day had only just broken, turning the sky pearl gray and sending the stars to sleep. It was quiet, the few sailors going about their tasks with silent ease. No one stared at him, or teased him.

They had been at sea for a week. So little time had passed since Prospero had raised a storm and snared a ship with his magic. And not just any ship. It was carrying Antonio, Prospero's usurping brother who had stolen the wizard's dukedom and cast him adrift at sea with Miranda. The King of Naples and his heir, Ferdinand, were also aboard. These noble men were accompanied by jester named Trinculo and Stephano, a foul, drunken butler. Caliban blushed with humiliation when he thought of these last two.

They were the first of the shipwrecked men to find him. He'd been gathering wood in the middle of the storm when the jester came along. Caliban thought he was one of Prospero's pesky servants come to torment him again. Ariel may have been the most trusted, but he was not the only spirit who served the wizard. There were many that seemed to delight in pinching Caliban while he worked. So when Trinculo appeared, Caliban tried to hide by lying down on the ground and covering himself with his rough cloak. Trinculo thought he was dead, struck by lightning, and crawled in under the cloak as well to shelter himself from the rain. That made Caliban flail about, thinking that he was about to be pinched and abused.

Stephano found them like that, shrieking and kicking beneath the cloak in the middle of the storm. He dealt with the situation in the way that he dealt with everything. He poured liquor down his throat, and for good measure poured it down Caliban's as well.

That drink had been like a divine nectar to Caliban. It filled him with boldness. The two stumbling men were his chance to win back the island. He called Stephano his god and convinced the drunken man to kill Prospero, promising him Miranda as reward. "Steal his books," Caliban told them. "He's nothing without them. Then drive a nail through his head. You will be the island king and we will be your servants."

Of course he planned to take it all for himself. But Prospero knew about their plot. One of his spying spirits had told him. Caliban, Stephano, and Trinculo were sent on a hopeless, floundering walk all over the island. The home he'd known all his life became foreign to Caliban, and Prospero's spells landed him in a bog with the two cursing men. When they finally found themselves at the hut, that drunken idiot Stephano had put on Prospero's clothes, playing at being a king. Before long spectral hounds chased them away. When the three of them could run no further, they fell to the ground and were instantly under the wizard's curse of twisting muscle cramps.

During that time Prospero worked on his revenge. By sunset that day he was reinstated as the Duke of Milan. A royal engagement between Miranda and Ferdinand was officially witnessed in the hut Caliban had built. Before abandoning the island Prospero broke the staff and drowned his spellbook in the sea.

But Caliban was not left behind. On the harbor shore Prospero had declared before everyone that Caliban belonged to him and that he meant to keep him. "This thing of darkness I acknowledge mine," were his precise words. They were far from heart-warming, but then Caliban had tried to have him murdered.

It had blinded and bewitched Caliban, that claim upon his soul. He had never dreamed of leaving his island. He did not desire the company of all these mocking men. When he had first come aboard they made him dizzy. They all looked like gods, with their straight limbs and shining teeth. But he was not so easily fooled anymore. He would never worship another human being.

And he saw his master differently too. Prospero's magic was gone. He seemed much older, and smaller, especially when he stood beside the one they called king. But Prospero would never be weak. And no one dared to tease Caliban when he stood in his master's shadow.

Soon they would come to this strange land filled with even more people. He'd heard Prince Ferdinand telling Miranda about it. People lived there together like a colony of nesting cormorants. He rubbed one of his bare feet against the other, warming it in the chill morning air. They would go to a castle, the prince had said. A great home, richly furnished. There would be fine food to eat, and servants to bring it to them.

His mother would be happy to have him in such a home.

He heard footsteps behind him. He turned, lowering his head and peering furtively. He'd learned that this was the way to attract the least attention. It was Miranda. She paused, then smiled, and continued toward him. "Good morning, Caliban," she said, resting her hands easily on the rail before them.

She looked like she'd lost her fear of him, no doubt because she was protected all around. She didn't need to worry. He had seen the horror and revulsion on her face when he had tried to make her his own. Prospero had been equally disgusted with him. "You tried to violate the honor of my child!" he'd thundered, before leaving Caliban imprisoned to a rock.

Remembering the wizard's anger, Caliban still marveled that the man had not killed him. His mouth twisted bitterly. Miranda had called him vile and brutish. Prospero had renamed him Hagseed.

But they still needed him.

So Prospero let him live, even though he had boasted, reckless in his shame, that he would use Miranda to fill the island with baby Calibans.

Yet here she was, seeking out his company. She behaved as

though there had never been any darkness between them, as though he was still her friend and teacher. He supposed his face, however loathsome she might find, it, was at least familiar.

"Are you frightened of it, Caliban?" she asked quietly, staring at the land ahead. "I am," she added, putting him at ease.

"Yes," he replied, simply. He was not ashamed of fear, not like the men of the ship. They ridiculed fear in themselves and others. They were afraid of being afraid, Caliban thought, and the silliness of that thought made him smile.

She saw his smile and misunderstood. "You don't seem to be," she said.

"I am, though," he answered. "I miss my island. I don't think I should have left my home."

"Father would never have left you there alone," she said.

Caliban did not reply. He did not mind being alone. He was far more bothered by these strangers.

"I worry about how I will seem to them. The people in the palace," she explained. "I'm used to such a simple life. Perhaps they will not think I am fit to be a queen."

He could see that she was troubled. "The people on this ship think you are," he answered. "You will do well. Everyone will like you."

She smiled at him, then reached out and squeezed his hand. The shock of her touch jarred him. He stepped back from her.

She looked embarrassed. "Thank you, Caliban," she said, awkwardly.

There were more footsteps behind them. He did not turn to see who it was. That confident stride could only be one person.

Caliban slipped away, around the other side of the deck, while Miranda turned to greet her lover. He heard Ferdinand reprimanding her for speaking with him. "He is as loathesome as a toad," the prince said. "His teeth are like scattered tombstones, falling over themselves in a neglected graveyard. I am sure he breathes a noxious vapour."

Such wit. He did not wait to hear her reply.

Prospero was still sleeping, his breathing deep, a gentle whistle coming from his nose as he exhaled. Caliban stood over him, tracing every familiar feature of the man's face with his eyes. He would never have dared to stand so close to his master on the island. But now there was no fairy to torment him. Now there were no spells to bind him.

And it was then he realized that he might go free.

The thought stilled his breath. He could slip away from Prospero. He could roam the world, see strange and wondrous places. He could be his own master.

Prospero stirred, rolled to his side, and slept again. Caliban knelt and stared at the hand that clutched the quilt. It was thin, the veins rising in lumps beneath pale flesh. He remembered this hand stretching out and stilling a storm. He remembered it turning the pages of his book, carefully pressing each one down so that it would lie flat. He remembered it resting on his daughter's shoulder as he taught her to read, tapping his fingers gently on her head when she mispronounced some word.

He reached out his own hand and briefly touched the tips of his fingers to those of this terrifying man. There was no shock. He pulled his hand away and stood up, once more looking down on the sleeping figure.

This once great wizard was going to lose his child, however happily. He was returning to a home that had rebelled against him. His power was gone, except for some small trifling magic that even a child might have.

Prospero would need him. Would want him by his side. Did want him, or else he would have left him back on the island with no further thought. He had always acted in his own interests, after all.

And it was good to be needed, to be wanted.

Caliban took a deep breath. He would stay with his master. It was what he chose to do.

"I will take care of you," he whispered. Prospero snored in response. He looked slightly foolish, with his mouth open like that. "Just like I have always taken care of you," Caliban added.

He lay down on the mat that was his bed. The ship rocked him. He stared out the small window at the swaying sky. Time slipped away, and he slept as well.

The next day they arrived in Naples. Before leaving the cabin Prospero clutched his arm. "Don't get any silly ideas about running away, Caliban. This isn't your island. You need my protection here, you understand?"

"Yes, master," Caliban said. He spoke gently, because he did understand. Prospero was more afraid than he or Miranda.

The former wizard looked relieved, then removed his hand and straightened his back. "Good then. Let's go," he said.

Caliban admired his courage.

II.vi.

Caliban stood to the left behind Prospero. His hood was drawn forward, masking his face with shadows. The other servants now called him "the monk." Well, that was an improvement over their earlier names for him: fiend, hell-lump, beast-man.

Ferdinand, now Prospero's son-in-law, was to take control of the dukedom. Prospero's dream of returning to civil life and taking up the reins of Milan's government had been a false vision. He was no better suited to mundane reality then he had ever been. Less so, after his long years on an island where he had lived by magic. Just seven months after his return, he began to disappear into his library for longer periods every day. At first it seemed that he tried to fight his own interests. But once he began the work of alchemy, he abdicated completely and sent for his son-in-law to replace him as duke.

The clatter of wheels on gravel grew louder. In another moment the carriage came around the corner of the drive and into view. There was a small escort of ten riders with it. That surprised Caliban. He'd been expecting a whole entourage.

The carriage drew up and servants sprang to work, opening the door and lowering the steps.

Ferdinand stepped down first, then turned to help his wife. Caliban felt his heart constrict. It had been nearly five years since he'd seen Miranda last, and in that time she had grown regal. No one but Caliban could imagine this tall, beautiful, stately person running barefoot and in patched clothes through the wilderness. But the smile and the warm greeting she offered her father were the same as ever.

Caliban lowered his gaze to avoid meeting hers. That was how he came to look straight into the pale, thin face of the three-year-old princess. Her hair hung in thick, lank braids on either side of her head. Her hazel eyes were large and fringed with impossibly thick lashes, making her appear not quite human. They stared at each other for a long moment. She was curious, fearless. And then she smiled at him, in her funny crooked way, a small dimple sinking into her left cheek.

No one had ever smiled at him on first sight. Caliban didn't move, afraid that he'd break the spell. The child was turned from him and introduced to her grandfather. "This is Chiara, of course," Miranda said. The little girl dipped a curtsey, her smile replaced with a solemn expression. "It's a pleasure to meet you, Grandfather," she said to Prospero. She sounded sincere, like the formal words were her own and not a rehearsed speech.

Prospero knelt down and took her chin between his thumb and forefinger. "Let me look at you properly," he said. The child waited, looking back at him calmly. "You'll do very well," he said at last. "Will you come and visit me each day?"

Chiara looked to her mother, who nodded. "Yes, I will, Grandfather," she said. "Will you read me stories?"

"Of course," Prospero replied. Then he patted the child's head and stood up. Caliban could feel the impatience returning to Prospero. He had been reading about salamanders when he was summoned to meet his daughter and the new duke, and Caliban knew how anxious he was to get back to the library.

State affairs never happen quickly. It took days before matters were settled enough for Prospero to retire back to his studies. During that time Caliban was kept busy gathering supplies for the upcoming work. Caliban was not sorry to be outdoors. He didn't like the uproar of the palace. The entourage had arrived, and the whole place was crawling with servants, both new and old, scurrying about with their arms full of clothes and curtains and dishes and papers.

So Caliban dawdled with his errands. On the fourth day after the new duke's arrival he was sitting in his favorite sunny spot in the kitchen garden, surrounded by the heady smell of herbs. He needed to gather more fennel, but he was in no hurry. Prospero believed the herb heightened his ability to think, so Caliban was forever brewing teas with it, and strewing it around the workroom floor. He didn't mind. He liked the herb himself. For a while he'd been trying to make a liquor out of it, but he hadn't had much luck so far. He thought a fennel wine would be a lot more useful to the world than the Philosopher's Stone, even if the stone was capable of turning base metals to gold and promised eternal life. But he kept that opinion to himself.

"This is a nice place," said a small voice. Caliban snapped his eyes open. There was the little princess, alone.

"Are you lost?" Caliban asked. His words came out like a bark, but the child did not flinch. "Where's your nurse?" he added, in what he hoped was a gentler tone.

"She was telling stories to someone," the girl replied. "I wanted to look around, but she kept telling me to wait. She likes to talk," she explained, "but I don't like to listen to her. She says mean things."

"Ah," said Caliban. He felt a bit helpless. Should he return the princess to her nurse? The woman would likely take one look at him and accuse him of kidnapping the child.

"Are you Caliban?" she asked him, breaking his unpleasant speculations.

"Yes," he said. "I'm your grandfather's servant," he added.

"Yes, I know," the princess said, nodding. "You're from the island."

"That's right," he replied. A sudden choking wave of home-sickness caught him. To conceal it, he bent down and pulled up three fennel plants.

"Those are funny," the child said, touching the double bulb roots with her fingers. "What do you do with them?"

"I eat them," Caliban said. "Would you like a taste?"

She nodded, her eyes wide. He snapped off a bit of stalk. "Pop it in your mouth," he directed. She did so, trusting him completely. The flavor made her smile. "It's good," she said.

"Your grandfather is very fond of it," Caliban said. "I'll make this into tea, and then—"

A scramble of feet and a cry of "Princess Chiara!" shattered their discussion. In a moment the garden was filled with breathless, panicking women. Miranda herself was among them. She was embracing her daughter when her gaze fell on Caliban. She stood, flustered. "It's you!" she said, then blushed deeply. "Forgive me, Caliban," she said, taking herself in hand. "This little scalawag likes to wander off. I'm glad she found you," she added. Politely. He did not think she meant it. She had pushed the girl behind her, after all.

"Caliban let me have some of his plant," the child said, pulling herself around her mother. "I liked it very much. Thank you," she said. Then she curtseyed. Her mother gathered her up and the flock of females left. Caliban watched them go.

He hoped Chiara would escape again, sometime soon.

II.vii.

"Father was very cross," Chiara said. "He yelled at me. He said, 'A royal princess does not carry vermin in her pockets!'"

"He's right about that," Caliban said. "I told you to let them go. You shouldn't make pets of wild things."

She stuck the end of her braid in her mouth and chewed on it. It was a habit that drove her nurse and mother to near distraction. "I know you're right," she said. "But I loved their sweet little paws and their black eyes. And they would sit up so prettily for a treat."

"Rats carry disease. Your little sweet things might have given us all the plague." He put down the mortar and pestle he was using and washed his hands carefully, as always, in the porcelain basin. Then he reached for the notebook. Prospero wanted everything recorded in detail. Caliban found the writing tedious, but enduring his master's lectures was far worse, so he gritted his teeth and did as he was told.

They were in his workroom, which was no more than a large closet connected to Prospero's study. Its order was set up and governed by Caliban alone. Prospero never came back here, nor did any other servant. Only Chiara ever joined him here. "My kingdom," Caliban called it. He was master in this small space with its one high window that let in light, fresh air, and the distant sound of the sea. Often he would pause and listen to the slap and sigh of the surf, hearing it more with his memory than with his ears. For a moment it would take him back to his island home.

There were shelves on all the walls, holding glass and porcelain and earthenware vessels. All of them were neatly grouped and displayed on the smooth oak boards that he kept oiled and gleaming. There were bunches of drying herbs hanging upside down from the ceiling, and baskets of dried ones on the floor beneath the shelves. These mingled their various perfumes with the musty scents of cork and clay to mask the sharper odors of tinctures and decoctions. Only one of the shelves was dedicated to Caliban's medicines. These he worked on tirelessly in the spare moments of his life. The healing and easing of the body's ills seemed to him a far more meaningful pursuit than Prospero's search for eternal life. Or spiritual transformation. Or the Philosopher's Stone. It was a constant complaint of Caliban's that not even the alchemist himself seemed to be clear about what it was he was searching for.

"You seem grumpy today," Chiara said. "Do you want me to write for you? I don't mind."

"Why aren't you at your studies?" he asked. Her offer of help irked him. Writing was the one task that made all his fingers turn into thumbs. He was determined to master it.

"Grandfather fell asleep," she explained. "I didn't want to wake him up to ask him for help."

The tip of the quill bent, sending a glob of ink across his words. Caliban stifled an oath. He got out his knife and went to work sharpening the nib once again.

"He was up late last night," Caliban explained. "Waiting for the furnace to cool."

"And?" she prompted. Caliban was certain he could see her ears perk up like a dogs. Alchemy had begun to fascinate her as well.

"And I just ground the result here with this pestle," he said.

She stared glumly at the charred powder in the mortar's bowl. "That doesn't look much like gold," she said.

"What a surprise," Caliban replied. He went back to his writing. Prospero would complain bitterly about that ink stain. Caliban could hear the old man's voice in his head. "Perfection, Caliban," he would say. "We must never accept less of ourselves than the very best. Otherwise the work will fail."

Caliban finished his notes and put away the notebook. "I need some air," he said. "Do you want to come to the grove with me?"

The grove was a small wood that grew by the castle. Three years ago, when Ferdinand had become King of Naples, Prospero had chosen to move in with his daughter. From the day of their arrival in Naples, Caliban had found refuge in the trees. Chiara often did the same.

"I'd better not," she answered with a sigh. "I'm trying to act like a lady right now, so that Father won't despair of me."

"I see," said Caliban. He knew – the whole castle knew – that the queen had suffered another miscarriage. Every time it happened the royal noose tightened around Chiara. At ten years of age she was still the only child. King Ferdinand could not afford to have a wild daughter.

"I wish Mother would have a son," Chiara said, speaking to Caliban's thoughts. She often did that.

"That is what we all wish for," Caliban said. "But in the meantime—"

"—I have to practice my sewing and my French," she sighed. "I'd rather catch toads."

"You could always kiss them and pretend you're looking for a prince to marry," Caliban suggested. He pulled on his boots. It had rained lately and the ground outside was muddy, even under the trees in the grove.

"You're so helpful," Chiara said. She grinned at him and tweaked his right ear.

They left together, walking silently past the snoring wizard propped in his armchair. In the hallway they parted. She went off to her drudgery of courtly manners, and he to his forest hideaway.

Outside the servant's door he looked back. She was watching him from her window. She waved to him, wistfully. He waved and disappeared into the wood.

Act Three

The Alchemist's Furnace

III.i.

His knees hurt in the morning, making loud popping noises as he bent down to stir up the fire for the day's work. Pausing for a moment, Caliban let the heat of the quietly crackling flames soften the movement of his hands. These he spread out before him, regarding them in the morning light. The flesh was pale, mottled with the purple marks that he had been born with, marks that spread like spilled wine over his shoulders and down his arms, with more splashes freckling his neck and face. These marks he barely saw anymore. What he did see was the skin thinning over the knotted bones of his long, deft fingers. He was growing old. Gently, he rubbed his hands together, reassuring himself that the muscles still held their skill. His hands had always been clever. Prospero had seen that from the very beginning.

"Caliban? Have you got that fire going?"

The old wizard Prospero appeared in the doorway, pulling his beard out from under the neck of his heavy silk robe and squinting at him with age-bleary eyes. Those eyes hid the sharpness of the mind behind them.

"Yes," Caliban replied shortly. It was the same greeting they had been giving one another every morning for twenty-eight years.

"Hmm. That's fine, then," the old man rumbled. He sat down, slowly and creakily, into the chair by the fire, adjusting his robe carefully. Then he put out his hand, palm up, as though begging. Caliban placed the leather-bound journal on it, then waited while the old wizard rifled through the pages of spidery writing. Finally he came to the last entry, which he glared at and mulled over for several minutes. Caliban waited further, standing as still and silent as a statue. It had become a game of his, this becoming stone. He counted it a victory every time people forgot he was in the room.

The old man looked up and said, "Right. We'll need to remake the cinnabar. There must be some impurities in the previous sample. Fetch the white queen from the back – and mind your hands are clean."

Caliban nodded and left, letting the reminder slide off him in the same way that mercury slipped across the surface of the table when it was spilled. The silvery liquid metal was always the "white queen" to Prospero, just as it was to all alchemists. Everyone who strove to discover the secret of immortality spoke in riddles.

"Fools in a fool's game," Caliban would often say to Chiara.

"The names have to be symbolic because the work is symbolic," Chiara would reply, always in the patient voice one used with a stubborn child. "The real change is supposed to take place within the alchemist, not the metal. You know that." Then she would grimace. Alchemy was the one subject they could never agree upon.

"Bah," he would say. "It's quicksilver to me. Names should be descriptive."

"Fine then, Sir Grumbleboots," she'd laugh. They would both laugh.

He went to his work room and performed the requisite hand washing. In the far right corner a low basket stirred and a cat stepped out and rubbed itself in calico splendor against Caliban's leg. He smiled, a rare and transforming expression of contentment crossing his face. "Good morning, Penelope," he said, giving the cat a quick and affectionate stroke on the head. "Was the hunting good last night?"

The cat purred in response. She stretched her front legs luxuriantly and extended her claws, then pulled forward and let the stretch glide over her shoulders and down her back, ending in a quick flicker of her tail's tip.

"Excellently done," Caliban said, giving her head another quick rub as he set her dish of water on the floor before her. She took a cautious sniff before she began to drink, as she always did. He was not offended by this lack of trust. It was the way of all cats, of all things wild, and he approved of it.

He straightened his back suddenly and frowned, sensing a new presence in Prospero's chamber. No one disturbed the old wizard at this hour, except perhaps—

"How goes the work?" The voice was quiet, deep. It always surprised people when they first heard Princess Chiara speak.

His smile returned, though it was tainted with some concern. To Penelope he said, "Our girl is back. She was not due till tomorrow." He picked up the flask of mercury and followed the cat back into the sitting room.

Chiara looked up and grinned at him in her funny lopsided manner, her wide mouth stretching up higher on the left side. Her face was all points and angles, framed by masses of heavy, dark hair. She looked as unroyal as ever.

Prospero broke off his querulous analysis of their recent failure and looked up at him as well. "Put that back," he barked, then turned to his granddaughter. "Never mind the work for now," he said. "Tell me about Milan."

"Milan seems changed," Chiara replied. "It's smaller, and stranger, than I remember it." She looked down at her hands, seemed about to say something more, then began to bite her fingernails. It was a habit she'd had from childhood. It meant that she was troubled.

Not just troubled. Caliban knew at once that there was something terribly wrong. But he did not speak. In Prospero's presence he was always a shadow. Instead, he waited. He knew the old man would not be long in asking the question.

"What's the matter?" Prospero stared at his granddaughter until she lowered her hand with a self-conscious laugh.

"My father..." She paused, searching carefully for the right words. "My father completed some negotiations with Spain."

Silence. "And?" said Prospero.

"And so I am to be married to a Spanish prince, in order that my father secure his position. Spain will be his ally." She turned her face away and looked into the fire.

"Spain!" yelled Prospero. "The Spaniards are lascivious mothers of dogs!"

Chiara laughed, her deep rumbling chuckle dissolving the sting of the words. "Now I know why father wanted to be far away from you during the negotiations."

Prospero's brow grew even more thunderous.

"It's not so horrible," she added quickly. "He is from a good family, Grandfather. I'm told they are very kind, very loving."

"Bah!" snorted Prospero. "Let them love each other and leave us to ourselves. Spain wants to eat us alive. Why would he make such an alliance?"

"He feels that if he makes Spain his ally then we will be spared from foreign rule. He says that in matters of state it is best to keep your enemies close. He says that I will be able to make many journeys home, in time. He says that it is a good match, and that I should count myself fortunate." She looked away into the fire again. "Regardless, it is done. I sail for Spain in a fortnight."

"A fortnight!" bellowed the old wizard. He half rose from his seat, then sat down again, his face slackening in shock. Caliban moved to his side, pressing his fingers upon the ancient, fragile wrist to find the pulse. The old man revived. "Off me!" he barked. Caliban stepped back and away. He knew his place.

"This shall not be," Prospero said, anger rasping the edges of his voice. "I have sway yet. I will not let you be sent so far from your home to an uncertain life in a foreign land. No, by God, I shall not."

Chiara's face twisted strangely. "Father is adamant, Grandfather. He knew you'd object, and told me not to look to you for help."

Prospero stared at her for a long minute. "So you have already asked to be spared from this marriage."

"My life is here with you. So is my work. Of course I asked to be spared." She glanced at Caliban, then gave a choking laugh and scooped Penelope into her arms. She buried her face in the cat's fur and seemed to draw strength from her. When she looked up again, her expression was calm. "I am a king's daughter," she said evenly. "My life is not always my own."

Prospero stared back at her, both of them shielding their emotions. Caliban watched them impassively, his own anguish pushed down and away. This was the way civilized people always behaved. They felt one thing and showed another. They wove fishnets of courteous lies and gasped out their days in traps of their own making. He realized, standing there, that he had become a master of the craft.

"Caliban," said the old wizard, "I believe the day is a fine one for collecting herbs. We'll see to the cinnabar later."

Prospero meant, "Get out." Caliban nodded and turned to go. Just before he left the room, however, he stole a glance at the princess's right hand. The fingers were crossed. He coughed once, softly, to show that he'd seen the signal. He would talk with her later, in the stillness of the night.

He shut the door behind him and hurried toward the

servants' stairs, grateful for this chance to escape outside. It had been a long time since he had been this upset. He must find a way to free Chiara from the Spanish prince.

III.ii.

Chiara watched her grandfather. *He's so old. Too old,* she thought. Aloud she said, "I'm glad now that my Spanish tutor was so good. If he'd been as terrible as my Latin one, I'd be in serious trouble." She forced a cheerful smile.

He saw through her. "Bah," he said again. "Your father is a fool."

She hugged the cat close to her chest, ruffling the fur around its neck. Penelope purred loudly, filling the room with comfort. "It is done, Grandfather," Chiara said wearily.

"Have you exchanged vows?" Prospero snapped.

"You know I have not."

"Then it is not done." He drummed his fingers furiously on the arm of his chair.

"It must be done, Grandfather," Chiara replied. "Father needs this. I can only be what I am and do my duty. Pity the poor prince," she added, her odd smile twisting her face once more. "What will he make of me, I wonder?"

"He'll make himself to be the luckiest fellow on earth," her grandfather retorted. But his words rang hollow. Chiara saw the truth written on her grandfather's face. The Spanish court would eat her alive.

She shook her head. "Let's ignore it," she said. "It's a stupid fate, so we'll pretend it doesn't exist. Tell me about the work. You were saying that there were impurities in the cinnabar. May I see your notes?"

"I'm so close to finding the agent of transformation," he said. "Once I have that, then I'll be able to help you, Chiara. I won't be so feeble. My powers will come back to me, I know it. I'll be able to do something for you, just as if I were on the island again. You'll see, Chiara. There must be something wrong with the white queen; everything else I am sure of: the black lead, the sulfur, the urine of an innocent boy… I have it all. But the white queen, there is something amiss with it. I've told Caliban many times, but still he brings me this inferior stuff. It has no potency, I am convinced. I think Caliban may be trying to spoil the work."

"No, Grandfather, he isn't. You can trust Caliban. You know that." She held his hand and stroked it, trying to calm him. He was often agitated now when he spoke of the work.

He seemed to read her thoughts. He was skilled at doing that, after all these years of shared secrets. "I'm growing desperate, Chiara," he admitted. "Time is running out for me. I don't mind so much for myself, but I can't fail you, Chiara. And now with this news…" Prospero ground his teeth in vexation. "I will find a way to save you," he promised.

She shook her head. "It is the way of the world, Grandfather. Don't be so frightened for me. I am stronger than you know. And you mustn't panic about the work. Rushing won't help. Let's be calm and go over the notes again. Perhaps today is the day when we'll make the discovery. Perhaps by tonight you'll be drinking the elixir of life." She smiled at him, and soon he smiled back. An alchemist lived by hope. They bent over the spidery handwriting, their brows identically furrowed, searching for the recipe for freedom.

III.iii.

Caliban lay on the cold stone floor of the tower gazing at the night sky through the window. He liked this narrow view of his heavenly brothers' dance. They moved across the window and away, in predictable fashion, night after night, shifting slowly with the seasons. Right now he was waiting for Orion. Joining the dingy walls and the ceiling was a tapestry of spider webs, and each night he had to brush away the mouse droppings before lying down. None of that mattered to him. This forgotten room had been a sanctuary for so long it seemed the most comfortable place in the world to him.

His ears caught the slight, muffled patter of footsteps on the stairs. He turned his face to the old oak door. It swung open silently. He always kept the hinges well oiled. The sound of creaking metal unsettled him.

"Just where I knew I'd find you," she said. He thought he could hear her smiling. "You should get a new robe, Caliban. That one is all tatters. Was it originally brown, or has it just become so over the years?"

"It suits me," he said. She lay down next to him, wrapping her skirts around her legs the way he'd shown her, long ago. It was important to stay warm.

"Tell me, Caliban," she asked, "why do you always smell like rosemary and cloves? Somehow, no matter what foul substance Grandfather has you working with, those are the only smells that stick to you."

He could feel her homesickness growing. He squeezed her hand and said nothing.

"Isn't he here yet?" she asked at last. Her voice was steady, now. She was determined to be brave.

"Not yet," he replied. "You should know that it's still too early."

"I always forget when Orion appears."

"You never bother to remember, you mean."

They both smiled. It was an old argument.

Caliban was her astronomy tutor. It had been her mother's idea, a way to appease the king over all the time they spent together. But Chiara waved off all his attempts to teach her the patterns of the heavens. It didn't bother him. She preferred to hear the stories of the stars, and he liked to tell them.

"Tell me about the dogstar," she said.

"Tell me about Milan," he replied.

She shifted her weight beside him, a small fidget of impatience. "There's nothing to tell," she said shortly. "Father met with several old men, they talked in circles and peered at me over the supper table. Then I became engaged to a prince in a faraway land. It's the stuff of stories, I suppose, only much more dull."

"It will not happen." He turned to look at her. She continued to stare out the window.

"It will not happen," he said again. "I would have seen it in the stars."

She laughed, short and sharp. "The stars," she said, "are notorious liars."

He chuckled. "Not to me, mousling. You know that."

The old nickname, born in her childhood, seemed to soften her. Chiara turned to him, her hazel eyes gazing into his.

"Do you truly believe so?" she asked.

"Truly."

She stared a moment longer, then turned her gaze back to the window. Her expression was troubled. "Father will be upset."

Caliban snorted. Father. The man barely spoke to his daughter now except on state occasions. Chiara had confided that she thought the king hated her for being ugly. She was undoubtedly right. He had been hated for the same reason all his life.

"That won't bother you, I know," she said wryly.

"Your life is not a state decision."

"It is. I don't like it either, but it is. And I'm too old now to dream about running off with gypsies or pirates."

He laughed at that. "Too old. Fifteen years this June and you're already decrepit. What is your father thinking, sending a child into marriage?"

"Child." She sniffed. "Mother was married at my age."

He said nothing.

"You're right though. It's stupid." She flipped over on her stomach and began to trace a crack in the stone floor with her finger tip. She did the same thing every night she came here. Caliban was certain that she'd worn it smooth at the edges.

"I don't suppose," she said, after a few moments, "that the stars have bothered to tell you what will stop the marriage?"

"Not precisely, of course."

"Of course." She grinned at him, lopsided mouth, lopsided humor.

"They tell of an adventure, and challenge."

"Pirates and gypsies after all, then?"

She laughed. It annoyed him. He was no crank palmist. Divination was his art and gift.

She must have seen his expression harden and realized that she had pushed too far. She sighed. "I think the idea that my small life is mapped out by the heavens is ridiculous, Caliban. The heavens are useful to sailors and storytellers. I don't want to go to Spain, but to avoid it I need a plan, not a vague promise."

"When do you sail?" he asked at last. There was no time for sulking.

"The twelfth, with the tide. Mother is rushing every seamstress in Naples to make me clothes fit for the Spanish court. Apparently that means a great deal of heavy velvet fabrics, no matter the climate." Her face twisted in a grimace. Caliban knew how much she hated any extremes in temperature. "Everyone tells me that Spain is a hot, dusty land, full of flies."

"You will sail." He frowned, puzzled by the riddle he was

reading in the sky. He needed to see more of the heavens than his window allowed. "There is danger. I will need to look longer. When I have observed some more I will know better."

"And I will practice my Spanish and hope for divine intervention." She stood up, shaking her plain dress into order. She always wore green and ignored the fashions of the day, dressing in simple, straight gowns with no adornments. It added to her odd appearance, and Caliban knew it made her mother despair. "I must get back. They're watching me closely these days to make sure I don't run away." Her expression was lost in the shadow of her hair.

He said nothing as she left, but turned back to the window. "Talk to me, brothers," he whispered. "Show me the way."

He stilled himself until his heart beat with the same pulse as the star that burned in the center of his view. "Speak to me of Chiara's fate," his mind whispered.

Light swept through him, a flood that crossed the heavenly seas and caught him in its tide.

—*She will be tested.*

Gooseflesh rose on Caliban's arms. There was something ominous here. It took all his concentration not to tremble, because that would break the link. "Will she live?" he asked. He hoped his question was absurd, wildly dramatic.

The light wavered, the color changed to gold.

—*Uncertain. There are many paths that branch for her, many possible outcomes.*

The star shone blue again and left him to join the dance once more.

He rose from the floor, slowly, his joints stiff and creaking. "Something must be done," he muttered. He drew his hood up over his head and walking swiftly and silently left the tower.

III.iv.

When Caliban returned to their shared chambers, he found the old wizard sitting in his chair by the fire, twisting a green silk handkerchief in his hands and muttering at the grate. He looked up. He did not even nod a greeting. "You shall sail with her," he said.

Caliban held himself in check, forcing his muscles to become stone even while his blood raced and cheered.

"The king will never allow it," he said tonelessly. "You know his opinion of me."

"The king will do as I say," the old man snapped. "He cannot refuse my dying wish."

Time stopped. Caliban felt himself growing small and speechless. "You are not dying," he whispered.

Prospero stared him. Finally he spoke, his voice flat but not ungentle. "I have never loved you, Caliban. I find it impossible even now, after all our years together. But Chiara does. She loves you, Caliban, and I know that you love her. You will protect her.

"As for dying," he added, his voice still steady, "I am. You know that I am, even though you deny it. The work has not saved me. I leave it to you, and to her, to find the transforming agent. If the two of you cannot do it together then it cannot be done at all."

Caliban took his turn at staring into the cold ashes. "I doubt that her royal Spanish husband will welcome either me as her servant or her preoccupation with alchemy." His kept his own voice level, calm. It seemed to come from someone else. This was a foolish hope. It was cruel for the old man to dangle this dream before him.

"Her royal husband be damned," the wizard barked. "That fool's fate is not for her. I will not see Chiara used as a royal bargaining chip." He broke off and stared at the knotted handkerchief in his hands. It seemed that he could not look up to say what needed to be said.

"Your life with me has not been easy, Caliban. There's been many a time that I thought it would have been kinder to leave you on your island. To leave you free and…. Well, no matter. We both made choices, and life's been lived. I was given a second chance. It seems only right that you should be given one too."

Caliban stood like a stump, his hands dangling uselessly at his sides. They had never been frank with one another. They had always communicated sideways, catching meaning from gestures and expressions. He did not know how to talk to this half-father in any other way.

Prospero lifted the handkerchief to his mouth and blew a word into it, then knotted it one last time. "It is done," he said, triumphantly. Or he would have said it, if he had any breath left with which to speak. He had none. He had simply mouthed the words. He grew pale and fell back into the chair. His hand holding out the handkerchief shook so badly that Caliban had to grasp the old man's wrist to hold it still before he could pry it from Prospero's fingers.

With the last of his strength Prospero pointed at the table. "Letter," he mouthed again, now with foam flecking his lips. His body spasmed and a rattle sounded in his throat. His eyes slid from Caliban's to the ceiling, then they emptied.

Caliban knelt beside the chair. He looked down at the handkerchief, clutched now in both his hands. It had been a wind spell, created with a life's breath. He had freed Chiara with a word.

He had freed them both. Because Caliban knew, even without reading the letter he saw lying on the worktable, that the spell would take them to the island.

He was going home. He sat for a while, staring at the form that had once been his master. He tried to feel something, but he could not. He had no emotions left. He felt as though he were a stranger to himself, as though he weren't actually living in his own body.

Finally he rose and collected the letter. He put it into his pocket, unread, and went to find the queen. He hoped that she would allow him to tell Chiara about her grandfather's last wish.

III.v.

The room still smelled like sulfur. The afternoon sun poured in its usual way across the tiled floor, splashing up the legs of the worktable and washing over its surface. There were glass vials filled with different fluids resting there that shattered the light into rainbow splinters on the walls. Chiara sat down in her usual chair, pretending that all was well, that her grandfather would appear from his sleeping chamber at any moment, muttering and cracking his knuckles over some particularly vexing thought. The silence deepened, grew longer. Chiara felt her mind letting go of its fantasy, felt the sorrow swell and take its place. Finally, her grief overwhelmed her. She turned her head into the cushioned back of the chair and sobbed.

She grew quiet and laid her face against the soft fabric of the chair. She neither lifted her head nor turned to look when she heard the door open and shut. It could only be Caliban.

There was a long pause, then her mother said, "Chiara."

Chiara startled, sitting upright and rubbing a quick hand across her face. Her eyes were swollen and a crease had been stamped across her right cheek where it had pressed against the chair. There were wild wisps of hair sticking out all over her head, while others were pasted to her forehead by its dampness. She jumped to her feet, smoothing out the skirt of her black dress. It was one of the new ones her mother had ordered to be made for Spain. She curtsied awkwardly. "Hello, mother," she said.

Queen Miranda was still beautiful. Her fair hair had darkened to the shade of late summer honey. Her skin was smooth and without blemish. A few faint lines around and between her eyes betrayed her age, but they were only visible in bright light. Her eyes themselves were blue and kind, though often troubled. "Sit down, Chiara," she said. She herself sat in her father's old chair.

Chiara stared at her mother. She had stared at her mother all her life, amazed that she was the daughter of this perfect woman. There was such a wide chasm between them that it took all their love to bridge it.

"It is a sad time, Chiara," her mother said at last.

"Yes," answered Chiara.

"But it is also a time of celebration," her mother added. She spoke stiffly. It sounded like she had trained herself to speak whatever she had come to say.

Chiara swallowed. "I had thought—" she began.

"I know what you thought," the queen interrupted. She stopped, perhaps surprised at the harshness of her own voice. She began again, her tone softer, but just as definite. "You think that your mourning will postpone your wedding. And so it should, all things being right and natural. But your father needs haste in securing this alliance. You must put your grief aside, Chiara, at least in the company of your new husband. I know it is a terrible thing that we are asking of you. I know how dearly you loved your grandfather. But you are a king's daughter, and your duty to your father and your country demands this price right now."

Chiara felt her face growing rigid with pain, with fury she could not express. No doubt her mother saw it. Miranda faltered for a moment, then seemed to steel herself. She pressed on. "You must not wear black to your wedding, Chiara. After the ceremony you may wear a black armband, but no more. It is as it must be."

Chiara looked down at her hands. She twisted them together in her lap to stop their shaking. "It is barbaric," she whispered.

"Chiara," said her mother warningly.

"I will do it, mother," Chiara said, still softly. "I will do it for the reasons that you give. But it is barbaric, and both you and my father know it."

"You are simply repeating what I have already said. But it changes nothing. It is still as it must be," her mother replied.

The door opened again. Caliban stood there, his hood drawn up. He stopped at the sight of the queen. "I beg Your Majesty's pardon," he said. He moved back into the hall.

"Stay," said the queen, rising from the chair. She walked to him and, amazingly, took his hand in her own. "I am sorry, Caliban," she said. And then, softly, so that Chiara could barely hear the words, she added, "He was your father as well."

Chiara saw a look pass between them, but she did not think her mother could read the darkness of Caliban's eyes. The queen dropped his hand and turned back to her daughter.

"My father asked the king to grant him a final wish," she announced. She could not keep the formal tone from her voice. Chiara was not surprised. There was nothing natural or easy in anything her mother was saying. "He knew his days were drawing to a close, and he wanted to make certain that Caliban was provided for."

Chiara caught her breath. She knew how her father felt about Caliban. "Mother, please—"

"Be still, Chiara," her mother said, interrupting her daughter once again. "My father asked that Caliban be allowed to accompany you to Spain, as your personal servant. The king thinks it is a preposterous request, but it was your grandfather's dying wish. I believe it is for the best," she said, smiling gently at Caliban.

Then the queen looked down at her hands. She looked embarrassed. It was a rare thing to see Miranda looking embarrassed. *She should be,* Chiara thought. *With everything she's said, she should be ashamed.*

"It pains me to say this," the queen began. Then she lifted her face and looked Caliban directly in the eyes, all her gentleness gone. "My husband and I ask only that you keep to yourself when you arrive in Spain. Do not allow yourself to be seen more than is absolutely necessary."

"Mother!" Chiara was mortified.

"I am sorry, Chiara. I find no joy in saying this. I am asking because it is in your best interest that this be so, and I know that

Caliban understands and will agree to it for the same reason. Your position in Spain will not be secure for some time. You must win your husband's good favor. Caliban's presence… Chiara, no matter how much you care for him you must know how others see him."

"They are idiots," Chiara said, flatly. She could not believe her mother was speaking this way about Caliban right in front of him, as though he were nothing more than an insensible tree stump.

Caliban waved his hand dismissively. He always claimed that he didn't care what anyone thought of him. "I understand, Your Majesty. I will be a shadow, and silent. You have my word."

She nodded. "Thank you, Caliban. That is that, then. Be well, Chiara." She left the room, her perfume lingering behind her.

III.vi.

Chiara stared after her, then turned to Caliban. "I am so glad," she said, at last. "Spain will not be so horrible if you are there. But I won't hide you, Caliban. People will think that I'm ashamed of you. They'll think that they can treat you badly. I won't have that."

"I will not be in Spain."

"What do you mean? Caliban, you won't abandon the ship and leave me?"

"I will abandon ship, but not alone."

Heat spread across Chiara's cheeks. "I cannot, Caliban. You must not ask it of me. If I run away, I dishonor my family and leave my father powerless."

"Powerless." Caliban spat the word contemptuously. "He is a king with great resources. He does not need to enslave his child to achieve his political goals."

"Stop it, Caliban. 'Enslave,' what a ridiculous word. He's my father. You know—"

"It is not ridiculous. It is the truth. And I know more than you understand. I know that your grandfather wished you to escape, and bought that escape for you with his very life."

Chiara's mind whirled. "What do you mean?" she asked hoarsely.

"He cast a wind spell with his breath. It took all that he had left. It will take us to the island, Chiara. There will be a storm. The sailors will believe us to be lost at sea. Your father will not be disgraced. He will simply have to look about for other means to further his ambitions."

"Don't speak about him like that," Chiara whispered. She stood and wandered about the room, her thoughts spinning. It was not honorable. Her parents would think she was dead. They would grieve for her while she fished for trout on Caliban's island. She stopped at that thought. It would trouble her father, but would he grieve? Her mother would, but her comfort would be found in small Ferdinand, their son. They would find another way to ally themselves with Spain. And she would be free.

"Let me think about it, Caliban," she said at last. "I will decide. Let me think."

She left the room quickly, unable to look at him. In her confusion she stumbled into a servant. The man caught her arm and steadied her, then stepped back and bowed. "The king wishes to speak with you, Highness. He's in his chamber now."

"Thank you," she said. She wanted to run out into the wood, but she steeled herself and walked the path of carpet-muffled hallways that led to her father.

She rapped softly on the door. "Come," said her father's voice from inside. He was always direct in his speech.

She entered by slipping in like a thief, letting the door slide shut again behind her. King Ferdinand stood alone by the window, gazing out across the south grounds. Chiara knew he could see the small grove of Caliban's trees from there. He called it the "Pagan Wood." No doubt as soon as they were gone, he would cut them down and put some pleasant garden walks in their place.

He turned and looked her over appraisingly. Chiara curtsied, then waited for him to speak. The king did not move from his position in front of the window. *That's all he is to me*, she thought. *He's nothing more than a dark silhouette in the shape of a father.*

He regarded her evenly. "You have spoken to your mother," he said.

"Yes," she replied.

He nodded. "I am sorry for the haste, especially at a time like this. But your grandfather understood the workings of state, however much he may have disliked them, and would have agreed with this course of action."

Hah, thought Chiara. She said nothing.

His mouth twisted, as though he could taste the lie and found it bitter. "It must be done, Chiara."

"So I was told by Her Majesty."

He heard the formal address. Chiara was never formal. It seemed to worry him. "You will obey?" he asked sharply.

"I will do what must be done," she replied.

He did not hear the evasion. It was a satisfactory answer. "Good," he said. He paused, casting about for the best way to end the interview. "Everything is in order, I take it, for your journey? You have no other needs?"

She looked away. "I have everything I require." She paused, then spoke again. "Caliban and I are taking grandfather's journals with us. I'm afraid you can't have them for the library yet."

The king frowned. "Your grandfather's obsession is dangerous, Chiara. You do not want to be called a witch."

"Alchemy isn't witchcraft, father. No doubt they understand that, even in Spain."

Her father's countenance grew darker. "I need this alliance, Chiara."

She moved her hand as though brushing away his objection. "I just want to have them, Father. I won't be using them."

He stared at her, searching for the truth. She looked back at him calmly. Finally, he sighed. "Take them," he said, shortly. "Just make sure your husband understands the work was Prospero's and not your own."

"Thank you," she said. It did not escape him that she made no promise.

Silence swelled between them.

"Is there anything else you would like, to ease your leaving?" he asked, awkwardly.

"Nothing."

"Ah. Good, then."

"Goodbye, father."

He laughed, without humor. "Good day, Chiara. It is not yet time for goodbye."

She smiled, sadly. "Good day, then." She curtsied again and left the room.

Tears burned her eyelids, but she would not let them spill over. She went to the star-gazing tower. It was odd to be there alone, odd to be there during the day. Everything looked smaller and dustier. She lay on her back and watched the clouds race across the sky. A bird, some sort of hawk, flashed in and out of view.

Chiara remembered the first time her father called her into his council chamber. It was shortly after she had started working with her first governess. She was only seven years old and completely terrified. The room had seemed cavernous, her father a stern giant. Why did she not attend to her lessons? He was told she was a clever child. Did she not like to learn?

"I do," she had replied, her lips white with terror.

"Then I don't understand." He frowned. She trembled.

"I want to learn new things," she whispered.

"New things? What do you mean, new things?" He looked puzzled, less irritated. It gave her some small courage.

"Teacher is having me learn my letters and the sounds they make."

"And what is wrong with that?" he asked, his frown returning.

"I know those things. I already know how to read. Grandfather taught me two years ago."

He had laughed then. She liked the memory of him laughing,

how he seemed suddenly so young and kind and generous. He had shooed her from the room, telling her that he would speak to her teacher, that all would be well.

It was the only time she remembered him laughing like that. The rule of Milan and Naples, consumed him, pulled him away from the smallness of her life. It pushed her here, to this tower, to Caliban.

Caliban, who had cleaned the dirt from her small scrapes. Caliban, who had listened as she described her nightmares and explained what they meant. He never told her to forget them. Caliban, who let her rage and storm and laugh and cry, never saying that she should not feel so, not behave so.

Any duty she owed to a father she owed to Caliban.

She would go to the island.

III.vii.

They stood together on the deck of the ship, both wearing hooded robes. Chiara knew it made her look like Caliban, and knew that bothered her parents. She looked down on them, standing together on the wharf, doing their best to look cheerful and mask their disapproval. It would be kind to pull back the hood and show them a respectfully tearful farewell, but she couldn't bring herself to do it. The hood's sheltering shadow was too comforting to leave.

It had been a difficult parting. None of them knew what to say. Her father had been nervous and stiff. She supposed that he was ashamed. He should be ashamed. Awkwardly he shook her hand – *shook her hand!* – goodbye. It killed her last, secret, ridiculous hope that he would change his mind.

At least her mother kissed her farewell. Then they had held one another for a long time, as though they could make up for all the empty years to come with one embrace. Miranda had whispered, "Be brave, Chiara," which had made them both cry. Chiara had stumbled up the ramp onto the ship, her vision blurred. Caliban waited for her on the deck, an unlikely beacon. As she stood there, she let the bustle of a ship getting underway distract her. Her tears dried.

"I do not feel sad anymore," she said quietly to Caliban. "I feel empty."

He said nothing. There was nothing to be said.

The noise and clatter increased. Ropes were thrown off and pulled aboard. The command to sail was given. Chiara raised her hand in farewell. Her parents did likewise. She turned away as the ship set sail.

"When do we loose the spell?" she asked.

"Let's go to our cabin," he said. "We can't stay out here on the deck."

Chiara looked around helplessly. "Do you know where it is?" she asked.

"Follow me," he said.

They stumbled past coils of rope and around sailors at work who moved out of her way politely. Nimbly. She felt like a great lumbering beast next to them. How could they walk so easily on a pitching floor? Finally she made it to their small cabin. Chiara threw herself down on the narrow bed. It was attached to the wall and floor of the cabin. She lay back and gripped the edge of it with her right hand, willing her head to stop spinning. "I don't think I would have made a very good pirate," she managed to say.

"There was never much doubt about that," Caliban replied.

She lay there with her eyes shut, praying that the tumult in her stomach would pass. It didn't. She opened her eyes to a squint and saw that Caliban was still standing. He was swaying. She shut her eyes again and said, "Sit down, Caliban. Please."

He sat on the room's only chair, a plain wooden one tucked under a rough writing desk. The desk was also bolted in place. Their traveling trunks were the only other things in the room. Gloomily, he looked at Chiara on the only bed. She opened her eyes in time to catch his expression. Forcing a laugh, she said, "I know. We've barely set sail and I'm already wretched."

"You don't look like you'll be moving from there for a while," he agreed. He pointed to a mess of net hanging on one wall, and a hook across the room from it. "That will be my bed." She pulled a face at his false cheerfulness. "Oh, come now. A hammock is a far sight better than the floor."

"Liar," she said. Her mouth filled with a metallic taste. She forced herself to swallow. "Are you going to cast the spell now?" she asked.

He reached into his pocket and grasped the handkerchief. "We haven't been able to talk much this past week," he began.

"My life has been one long dress fitting." She rolled onto her side, wincing at her stomach's sudden protest. "I had to stand there and watch those poor women be bullied. They made me twelve new gowns. Twelve! And for nothing. At least I managed to get a good pair of boots out of it all. I told my father that Spanish women are wild about riding horses."

"They are?" he asked.

She kept chattering, pushing against the pillow that seemed

to be filling her head in the place of her brain. "I don't know. I just wanted to get a good pair of boots. I don't suppose court slippers will be much use on the island." She looked at him anxiously.

"Chiara," he began. He stopped, as though he didn't know how to continue.

"I know," she said. She sat up gingerly and tucked her feet in under the skirt of her gown. Her wretched lavender silk gown, the not-mourning gown. She'd have to switch to her regular green dress, just as soon as the world stood still again. "I know that you're worried about how we'll manage on the island. I mean, how I'll manage. I am scared, Caliban. But I know that no matter how hard it is, it'll be better than being married in Spain."

He looked at his hands, and she followed his gaze. "You're strong, Caliban," she whispered. "And I am too. We'll be fine."

"We'll have to be," he said. "Chiara, are you sure? We'll have to build a house. We'll have to cut trees and split them into boards. It will take a while, and until it's done we'll live roughly. Even when it is done, we'll live roughly. We'll have to hunt for food, and if we don't find it, we'll go hungry."

A bitter smell pinched her nostrils. "I know all this, Caliban," she snapped. "I have thought about everything. I'm not a hot-house princess."

"I'll die, Chiara. Someday. Then you'll be alone."

An acrid taste furred the surface of her tongue. "I like being alone," she said. She wished with all her being that she was alone right now.

Caliban looked only partly relieved. "The stars…the stars told me something." He stopped.

"What did they tell you?" She lay down again wishing, praying even, that the ship would stop moving.

"They told me that you'll face a challenge. That you will be tested."

She glanced up at the round cabin windows. They looked as though they were sealed. She'd give a good deal for some fresh air. Caliban was making no sense. Her mind was full of babble. "Of course I'll be tested. This bloody ship is a test." She breathed to steady herself and forced a wan smile. "We'll be fine." She swallowed, then swallowed again. Her throat was strangely tight.

"My brothers weren't speaking about loneliness or hunger. The island holds some particular danger for you."

Beads of perspiration were prickling her forehead. One of them slid down into her left eye. She blinked it away. "Caliban, what are you talking about? You aren't making any sense."

He squinted at her. "Are you ill?"

"I'm fine. I'm just warm, that's all. What are you saying?"

"I'm saying that perhaps we should go to Spain."

She stared at him blankly for a moment. Then she leaned over and vomited on the cabin floor.

III.viii.

Caliban was a natural nurse. He wiped her face with a soft cloth, unbuttoned the now-ruined lavender gown, got her nightgown from her travel trunk, and then slipped out of the cabin for water and a mop. He supposed they had such things on a ship. Weren't sailors always "swabbing" the deck? He ran into a boy, no more than twelve years old, and explained what he needed. The fellow was puzzled. Caliban realized that he didn't speak Italian very well, so he tried again with simple words and gestures. Then the boy seemed to understand. He grinned and ran off. In a moment he was back with a bucket and bundle of rags. Caliban thanked him and went back to the cabin.

Chiara was in bed, huddled miserably under the rough blanket. The lavender gown had been tossed down on the floor, covering the mess of sick. She lifted her head briefly when he came in, making sure that it was him and not someone else.

"I'll get this tidied away in no time," he said, reassuringly. "As for the gown..."

"Throw it overboard. Really. I never want to see it again." She buried her face in the pillow and groaned.

He shrugged and used the gown to mop up the worst of the mess. Then he scrubbed the floor clean. "I'll be right back," he said, and disappeared out of the cabin once more. He propped the door open slightly so that some fresh air would blow in and chase the foulness away.

He dumped the scrub water and the gown overboard. The sight of Chiara's dress sinking beneath the waves made his heart clutch. *It's nothing,* he told himself. *It's just a useless dress tossed away.* But his mind kept returning to the vision of Chiara tumbling down into the sea.

She was afraid of water. She had been ever since she was a small child, screaming her way through every bath, no matter how her nurse coaxed and coerced her. Caliban had taught her to swim, thinking that would help. It had, but only to some degree.

Now he wanted to take her to his island, where the sea would surround her and hold her captive.

He went back to the cabin and set the bucket down beside her bed. "Just in case you need it," he said.

"In case?" she groaned. She flipped over and stared up at him. He smiled and stroked her forehead, letting his water-chilled hand cool her. She reached up and grabbed it with her own. "I don't care about your star brothers' danger, Caliban. I've made my choice."

She let go of his hand and rolled onto her side. She retched once again. When she was finished she gave Caliban a pale smile and passed him the bucket. "I'm sorry, Caliban," she said.

"It's nothing," he said. "Even sailors get seasick when they first leave port." He took the bucket outside and emptied it overboard. Then he found the boy again and managed to make him understand that he wanted a flask of drinking water. The fellow laughed out loud this time, but fetched a leather flagon as quickly as if he'd had wings on his feet. "Thank you, Hermes," Caliban said. The nickname surprised the boy and seemed to please him. He grinned again and was gone.

Chiara took the drink gratefully. "I wish my head would stop spinning long enough to let me think," she complained.

"In a few hours you'll be used to the pitch of the ship."

"A few hours!" she groaned. She buried her head in the pillow again.

"It will pass," he said. "For now, rest. Perhaps tonight I can talk to the stars once more and see if there's anything new to learn."

She threw up again. He sighed and patted her arm. There wasn't much else he could do.

Finally she slept. He went outside. The sky was beginning to darken. He lay down on the deck beside the cabin, out of the wind. The ship rode the gentle swells. The stars began to show themselves, but the movement of the sea made them seem to sway and veer from their course. He found it hard to concentrate. Without his window, the heavens were too distant and unruly for him to attract his brothers' attention. Added to that, the sailor on watch kept shuffling by, staring at him curiously. He finally gave up and went back inside the cabin.

Chiara was sitting up in bed, eating some dry bread he'd left for her. She looked almost cheerful, despite her wild hair and rumpled nightgown. "Any news?" she asked.

He shook his head and sat down with a snort of disgust. "I can't get my bearings on this ship. The stars shift about and are too busy with each other."

"Oh well." She was open about her lack of faith in his brothers.

"You're the only alchemist in the world who doesn't see the importance of the heavens," he said.

"Agreed," she admitted. She seemed herself again. "Spain is real, Caliban. The danger—"

"Is real. And deadly. Whatever Spain may be, it isn't that."

She began to chew her fingernails. "You never know," she argued. "Some royal wives get their heads cut off. Look at England."

"That's cheery," Caliban said. But an icy fist had closed itself around his heart. Perhaps there was no safe place for Chiara.

She sighed and took her fingers out of her mouth. "I'm just being realistic, Caliban. Your stars said I will be tested. They're right. Whatever I do, they're right. I'm not afraid. We'll go to the island."

Caliban stood. "You are convinced?"

"Yes. Do it." She picked up her bread and began to munch on it again.

Caliban went outside and pulled the handkerchief from his pocket. It seemed like such a ridiculous little wisp of cloth to put their hopes into. He held it for a moment. Magic. He hated magic. "This will be the last spell," he promised himself. Then, swiftly and deftly, he untied it. There was a faint sigh. Prospero's breath, Prospero's wish.

Caliban retied the knot tightly and pocketed the handkerchief. In a dark corner of his mind he felt it might still have some power. Power that he might need again.

The sky blackened and the stars were erased. It was as though an immense curtain had been drawn across it. Wind screamed around the masts and clawed at his cloak. Sailors yelled, but their voices were ripped and tossed to the sea. He staggered toward the cabin, wishing that he could calm the terror around him. It was always like this with Prospero's storms. They frightened the wits from every man and never harmed even a single soul. "All bluster, even to the very end," he muttered. And then, suddenly, his heart broke as fiercely as the storm. Prospero was dead. His father was gone. Blindly he made his way to the cabin door and managed to shut himself in, just as the first lashings of rain hit the deck. He lay down on the floor and howled his grief.

Chiara stared at him. The wild pitching of the ship made her cling to the sides of her bed. A huge wave swept across the deck and threw itself against the wall of their cabin. It threatened to send them to the deeps. Caliban was sure that it was trying to take Chiara away from the safe, regular world; take her away from him.

"Caliban?" she said. He could hear that now she was afraid. "Caliban, now isn't a good time for you to go mad."

"I'm all right," he answered. But that was a lie. Though he managed to stifle his raving, it did not take long before he also succumbed to seasickness. Chiara had already lost every bit of the bread she'd eaten when Caliban began to retch as well. He crawled over to her, and they both took turns clinging to the small bucket. Life seemed very grim.

After a time he grew numb, and he began to spend his time between each bout of illness remembering the fresh breeze that constantly blew over the stones and through the trees of the island. He thought of the small groves that were home to rare birds. He thought of the cold stream that ran thick with fine pink-fleshed fish returning from the ocean to the place of their birth. Then he was wrenched again by another bout of sickness, and he thought only of living to the next moment.

The storm raged for three full days. Fear and fatigue numbed everyone on board. When they slept it was shallow and punctuated by strange violent dreams. Every soul on the ship made ready for death.

And then it was over, suddenly and completely. The ship drifted into a harbor. The anchor was dropped. Sleep, healing and magical, fell upon the entire crew. Many simply lay down and slept on the deck, in the very spot where they had been standing.

"Will they be all right?" Chiara asked. She stood beside Caliban, surveying the fairy-tale scene around them.

"They will be fine," he said. "The magic had a kindness in it."

"But after they awake, Caliban…they'll know where we've gone, won't they?" She chewed her lip. "Won't they just come after us?"

"No." He gave her hand a comforting squeeze. "The enchantment carries a false memory within it. They will all dream that we were lost at sea. Together they will vouch that you were swept overboard in a sudden wave, and that I dove in after to save you."

Chiara smiled wryly. "You come off as quite the hero."

He grinned. "Noble in death," he replied.

They looked around. Fog obscured their view of the island, but they could hear the gentle lapping of waves against the shore. "We're very close to land," Chiara said softly. The combination of the spell and the mist made the world an eerie place.

"Yes," he said. He could smell it, taste it in the air: the land of his birth. But there was a strangeness, too. Somehow he felt that he was not welcome, that the island itself was angry and had turned its back on him.

He whistled, a lonely, thin sound like the distant cry of a seabird. The wind stirred around them, drawing away the mist.

And they saw the island.

Act Four

The Night Sea Journey

IV.i.

It looked like it had been burned and broken by some careless giant. Where there had once been groves of trees, there were now charred skeletal spears jabbing at the pale sky. The ground was blackened, the rocks split and cracked. The only sign of life was a dismal raven sitting on a twisted branch. It croaked when it saw them and flapped away, disappearing with dull wing claps into the mist. The air that wafted from the shore was sour.

"We've come to the wrong place," Chiara said. She looked at Caliban anxiously. This was clearly not the island of sweet airy breezes her mother and Caliban had always spoken of.

Caliban looked as tortured as the land. "It's the right place," he said, dully. "It's just all wrong."

"What could have happened, Caliban? A fire of some sort?"

He shifted his shoulders wordlessly. His face was pinched, his birthmarks purple against the ashy pallor of the rest of his skin. She turned her gaze back to the shore.

"Should we…" Her voice trailed off. What choice did they have now? The spell had been cast, the path had been chosen. Had she really expected to walk away from her life so easily? She stared at the wasted shore. They'd been prepared for hardship, but this was a land of death. She glanced at Caliban once again. He seemed shrunken, old. *It's hurting him*, she thought.

"We have to make it better, somehow. We have to make it right." She wasn't sure exactly what she meant, only that she would do anything to take away Caliban's pain. She tucked her hands inside her cloak. They were cold, but she knew that wasn't why they had begun to shake. "How do we get there?" she asked. She tried to make her voice casual, carefree.

Caliban pointed toward the ship's boat, lashed to the deck, upside down. "In that," he said.

The boat was made of oak boards, built to carry twenty men. Chiara doubted that she and Caliban would be able to budge it, let alone lower it into the water. That meant swimming to the shore. Chiara glanced at the dark waves of the deep harbor. The water looked cold and dangerous. *Probably shark infested, too,* she thought. She could hear it lapping at the sides of the ship, hungry for her life. The very thought of going into it choked the breath in her. She gripped the rail, her knuckles turning white. Resolutely, she held her voice steady and said, "We'll never move that boat, Caliban. We have to swim."

Caliban turned to her. It was clear that he saw through her mask of bravado.

She tried to smile, but found it impossible. She resorted to reason, convincing herself more than Caliban. "Besides, what will we do with the boat once we get to the shore? The captain will know someone deserted the ship. They'll come after us."

"They'll have to swim," Caliban said. "No sailor swims. And we could hide the boat, pull it up on shore and…" He stopped, his argument obviously pointless. They wouldn't be able to lift it over the deck, let alone drag it up the beach.

Chiara took his hand and squeezed it, as though he was the one who needed reassurance. "We'll have to swim, Caliban. There's no help for it." Then she let go of his hand, because her own had begun to shake again. She wrapped her arms around herself and pretended to be chilled.

She could tell from his expression that she had not fooled him.

And then, while she gathered her courage, the air seemed to thicken around them. She heard a sighing – like strange and distant lilting music. Right before them the light twisted into a rainbow whorl that suddenly took human shape. The creature was no taller than Chiara, and even more slender. It looked at them with almond-shaped, purple eyes, the pupils of which were slitted like a cat's. It stood in the air as easily as they stood upon the deck.

Caliban took one step away, and then stopped. He hunched beneath his cloak, seeming to dwindle before Chiara's eyes. For the first time she saw that his strength might fail him. A sudden burst of protective anger bolstered her flagging courage. She would not let Caliban be diminished. This stranger could be only one person. "Ariel," she said. Then, overcome by curiosity, she reached out and touched his arm.

It was not flesh. It felt like water, only her hand was dry after it passed through the creature's substance. The touch raised goose pimples on her skin and raised the fine hairs on the nape of her neck. Something had swept through her: a current of magic. Ariel pulled his arm away. She let her own drop.

"You are Prospero's kin," he said flatly.

"Yes," Chiara replied. "How did you know?"

"I was bound to the wizard for fourteen years. I know his blood." He stared at her for another moment with his strange violet eyes, then turned his gaze upon Caliban. "So you have returned, earth-man."

"Yes," said Caliban.

He was still hunched beneath his cloak. He looked shuffling, lumpen. Chiara wanted to shake him, tell him to be proud. She glared at Ariel.

"And you brought a new master with you."

Caliban flushed, making the purple birthmarks on his face almost black. Chiara knew he was furious. He straightened his back and squared his shoulders. "I have no master," he said, his voice low and rough. "I am a free man."

"Then a man with a mistress?" the creature asked. He smiled, cruelly.

The words made Caliban wince. Chiara flared again at the sight of his embarrassment. "Caliban is my friend," she said.

"You've grown bitter, Ariel," Caliban said, taking her hand and giving it a thankful squeeze. "You were often spiteful before, but you were never vicious."

"I've discovered that I'm a heartless being," the spirit replied.

He laughed dryly at his own joke, but no one joined him.

"Why are you here, Ariel?" Chiara asked. "You were freed by my grandfather over fifteen years ago. Why haven't you left?"

The creature glowered at her. "I was always free, Prospero-girl, whatever your grandfather thought. And I did leave. I wandered through your human lands and saw how you people destroy each other and everything around you. So I returned. This island is one of the last magic places left on the Earth. It is, as much as any place can be, my home. Why are you here, Prospero-girl? Have you come to enslave us all again? Or have you come to finish the great work of destruction that your grandfather left behind?" Ariel glanced at the island, briefly. "It may be for the best," he added bitterly.

"What are you saying?" Chiara asked. "Are you suggesting that it was my grandfather who did this?" She threw her arm wide at the wasteland before them.

"Suggesting?" Ariel shifted his shoulders carelessly. "The land is dying," he said. "And it was Prospero who dealt the death blow."

"How? Why?" whispered Caliban.

"You need to ask?"

Caliban gestured hopelessly. "I need to ask," Chiara said.

"Wizards," snapped the creature. He moved closer to Caliban, his whole being dangerously spitting flames. "The life of the island was taken and held by Sycorax, this earth-fool's mother. When she died, it moved to this," he stared at Caliban, "her hag spawn, though he did not honor it. Then Prospero came and took it for his own. You gave it to him, clod-waste.

Before Prospero left, he broke it. It has been bleeding away ever since."

"What are you talking about?" Chiara asked. "What life did my grandfather take?"

Caliban stared at the fiery creature. "The staff," he said.

Ariel nodded, snorting contemptuously.

"The staff, Caliban?" Chiara asked.

"Your grandfather had a wizard's staff when he lived here. He did all his magic with it. He found it here. It was my mother's. She made it from the island's guardian tree. Long ago," he said. His voice wavered and he looked down at his own hands.

"Found? Found? It was given to him, given by you, monster. The island's power," Ariel snapped. "The island's life." He burned brighter, making Chiara squint. But she would not turn away.

"He told me about that, about his staff and how he broke it. He was proud he'd done that," Chiara said.

"Proud!" The spirit burned so brightly Chiara did not understand how there could be anything left of him at the end of his anger.

Her grandfather had told her the staff had made him reckless at times. "I knew it would destroy most of my magic, but I broke it anyway. Never let anything control you, Chiara," he had said. "If anything comes to rule your life, you must let it go. Desire can bind as tightly as fear. Walk free of both."

"He didn't understand," Chiara said, slowly. "He didn't realize what breaking the staff would do. I'm sure of it."

No one said anything.

"I'm sure of it!" she repeated.

Caliban nodded, but he did not look convinced. "He had no love for the island, Chiara..." he began, then faltered. She couldn't hide her sense of betrayal. How could Caliban think her grandfather would hurt anyone or anything?

"He couldn't have known what harm it did, Caliban. If he even suspected it, he would never have sent me back here."

"That is true," Caliban agreed. His expression lightened.

Chiara felt more hopeful. "The staff is still here?" she asked Ariel.

The creature eyed her suspiciously. "It is," he said, finally. "It lies abandoned in your grandfather's hut, where he threw it before he left."

Chiara turned to Caliban, excitedly. "Perhaps we can mend it, Caliban. It would heal the island if we could, wouldn't it?"

Ariel stared at her. "It can only be healed by three magics working together: wizard, wild, and island. It will take a great deal in the spelling." The spirit shifted his gaze to Caliban.

Chiara saw him stiffen. This was a bad time for him to be stubborn about doing magic. "We can do that, can't we Caliban?" she asked him. She hoped he could hear the pleading in her tone.

"I will stand for the island," Caliban said slowly. "It is part of me. It is my land."

Chiara just barely managed to stifle the impulse to cheer out loud. "So we need wizard's magic. And wild." Chiara bit at her fingernails. She glanced at Ariel. It was unlikely there was any magic more wild than the fiery rainbow man. Surely he would help them, if it meant restoring the land. But a wizard?

Her grandfather had always said she had the gift. Chiara had never believed him. She didn't feel magical. Nerves twisted in the pit of her belly. "I guess that will have to be me," she said lightly. She did not feel light.

"Of course, you," said Ariel. "You have it in your blood. I felt it. But it is untried. It will not suffice for the spell-making."

The blood began to hum in her ears. "Well, what can I do?" she said. "There must be some way I can ready myself. Some sort of test," she said, poking Caliban gently in his ribs. He did not smile.

But Ariel did, and it was a terrifying sight. "Oh no," Caliban said. Chiara glanced at him anxiously. The mist had lowered around them again, swirling, filling the air with threat. For an instant it cloaked her, and she could see nothing. Then it cleared again.

"There is only one way," said Ariel. "You will need your grandfather's book."

"His book," said Chiara. "He threw his book into the sea."

Ariel nodded. His eyes glittered; his whole being seemed to shimmer with glee. "You will have to get it," he said, tasting the effect of his words. "It lies in the sea, five fathoms down, beneath the claws of the Leviathan."

Chiara turned to Caliban. "Well, at least it isn't Spain," she said.

IV.ii.

They stood on the rocky land spit of the southernmost tip of the island. Ariel had brought them from the deck of the ship, his magic carrying them in a brief but terrifying whirlwind. Chiara flung herself onto the ground until the world stopped spinning around her. "Can't you just magic yourself to the bottom of the sea and bring the spellbook back for me?" she'd asked.

Ariel stared at her, burning with a chill-blue flame. "My domain is the air," he said flatly. "Regardless, the task is yours. You may avoid it, of course. Go back to your life and leave the island to its death. It is what Prospero did, after all."

Chiara stood up and brushed herself off. It was madness, this plan of theirs. She should just let the island die. She should get back on the ship, go to Spain, marry a prince, and raise a brood of children. That was a real life.

She'd rather die.

"I wasn't serious," Chiara said, finally answering the spirit.

She smiled half-heartedly. "I was hopeful, but not serious. Nevermind. I'm ready."

She wasn't, of course. No one could ever be ready for what she was about to do.

The Leviathan. The great eternal serpent that surrounded the world. The ancient monster of the deeps. Chiara had seen countless drawings of him during her study of alchemy. She believed he was a metaphor.

She was wrong. *Don't faint,* she told herself. *Don't faint.*

Ariel's purple eyes gleamed maliciously. He could smell her fear, Chiara was sure. Not that he needed to. Her terror was written on her face, obvious in the shaking of her hands.

In the shaking of her entire body.

"Close your eyes," Ariel said.

She did as he commanded and was suddenly thankful that she'd been seasick for three days. If it weren't for her empty stomach, she'd be ill. It was bad enough that her fear made her almost witless. She couldn't stand being humiliated by it as well.

A warmth pressed against her face. She smelled strawberries in the sunshine. Then, all at once, she could not breathe. Her eyes flew open and stared into the strange violet ones of Ariel.

The spirit smirked. "You'd best get under the waves," he said.

She gaped at him, her blood beginning to thrum in her ears.

"You'd better hurry," Ariel said, his voice seeming to come from across a great distance. "You can no longer breathe air."

Caliban snatched at her arm before she threw herself into the foam. "You can do this. I have seen it in the stars."

Liar, thought Chiara.

She wished she could look brave and wise, but it was hopeless. Closing her eyes, Chiara plunged beneath the surface, throwing down her body before she could think anymore about what she was doing.

It was cold and dark and smothering and heavy. She slid downwards to the deeps, pulled by the undertow and by some charm woven into Ariel's magic. Seaweed caught at her, but could not hold her. She was twisted and tumbled, yet still she managed to live. All at once she stopped, and found herself lying on the bed of the sea, pressed there by the weight of many waters, wondering why she was not dead. Her lungs screamed for air, her throat burned, her head pounded to the drumming of her heart. She gasped, and saw her last breath rise away from her, a quicksilver orb, a bubble of life. Oblivion beckoned her as a warm embrace. She gulped her certain doom.

And she breathed. The water carried life to her, borne on the back of Ariel's spell. The sea had become, for this small time, her home. She lifted an arm and stared at her hand as it moved through the water, assuring herself that she had not been changed into a fish. The wild magic within her began to sing its mastery. Her flesh glowed softly, casting a pale light. She stood up, marveling at the weightless feel of her body, and examined the strange world around her.

There were wide expanses of sand stretching out in all directions, save where the land rose up like a mountainside. She realized this was the island's root. There she saw patches of sea plants. Some were low and scrubby, others clumped like underwater shrubs, and some waved long leafy fronds up into the heights of the ocean. She could see the path her body had torn in the silt already being covered by the shifting sand. A lobster crept across her foot. She yelped and kicked it away. It waved and snapped its claws, but it did not pinch her. She supposed that the magic protected her from injury. She hoped it would help her against the Leviathan as well. Remembering Ariel's expression she let that hope die.

Other creatures were drawn to her light. There were strange fish that gleamed with a luminescence of their own. Dark predators slid about the outskirts of shadow and gloom and stared at her with flat, blackened eyes that did not blink and showed no thought. She fought back her returning panic and began to walk, directed by instinct, to the coldest reaches of the sea. She sensed the great pulse of the Leviathan, beating slow and heavy beneath the waves, circling the earth, its own tail held between its jaws. It was a living noose, a deadly embrace. It had been that way since time began and would be so when it ended.

And resting there, between its giant clawed hands, was the spellbook of Prospero, now a treasure of the sea. In her mind she could see it, could feel the draw of its power. It was hers for the taking.

IV.iii.

Caliban stood upon the shore, staring at the silvery trace of bubbles left upon the surface of the waves. They were disappearing quickly. "Chiara's breath," he thought to himself. He looked up at the glowing spirit before him. "Your spell had better work," he growled.

"Or what, moon-calf?" Ariel taunted.

It was an old insult. It dwarfed him, made him a slave once more. Caliban grit his teeth. "Or she will die, and so will the island."

Ariel looked at him briefly, then shrugged. "My spell will work," he said. "She only needs to return by this same time tomorrow, and all will be well."

Fear tightened its grip on Caliban's heart. "What happens if she doesn't return by then?" he croaked.

"All spells fade," Ariel said lightly. "She'll drown," he added unnecessarily. "Or she'll be crushed by the weight of the water."

Caliban stared out at the sea.

"It isn't my spell you need to worry about, Caliban. It's the Leviathan."

Caliban swallowed every response he might have made. Ariel was only too right.

This was her decision, he told himself. *Never mind the fact that she's only fifteen and dutiful to a fault,* another thought replied.

"Cheer up, Caliban," Ariel replied. "I doubt that anyone of Propero's line could fail to get what they want." The spirit disappeared with a small thunderous clap of sound. Caliban sat down upon a rock to wait. He stayed there, a huddled lump, waiting for his child.

The hours passed, and Caliban did not move. Finally it grew late. Caliban could no longer feel his legs. They had long since grown numb from the chill of the rock. Still he sat, waiting, hoping that the surface of the blackening water would break and reveal Chiara, alive and well. But the water only moved in small, listless waves that sucked and spat at the sea's edge. Then, as dusk crawled around him, it began to rain. It was a sharp, needling rain that peppered his skin.

Caliban hunched his shoulders protectively, but he knew that he could not last much longer out in the open. He ground his teeth in anger. "This rain," he hissed, "smells of Ariel's magic."

Knowing that changed nothing. He could not stay on the rock in the open air any longer. His bones protested too fiercely to be ignored.

He stood, staggering slightly as his stiffened muscles and joints groaned about the change of position. The wool of his clothing was soaked through, its heaviness pressing him down.

The weight of water, he thought. Then he tried to think of something else, but that was ridiculous. There was nothing else to think of except Chiara, under all that ocean.

He could not help her by perishing of cold. She'd be furious if she rose triumphant from the sea to find his stubborn corpse sitting on the shore.

The thought almost made him laugh. Almost. "I'll tell her that," he said out loud, daring fate. "I'll tell her when she comes back."

But for now he knew where he would go.

The ground was slippery, the murk beneath the trees almost impenetrable, yet Caliban's feet followed memory across rocks and through brush. At last they came to a sheltered dip, a tiny valley of sorts, where the wind did not tear at his face and hair and clothing. Here, in this safe spot, the rain seemed to fall gently. And here, just where it had always been, was the hut that had been home to Prospero and his daughter Miranda. So many years ago. He stood for a moment in the gloom, gathering his courage. There were many ghosts to face here.

It was decrepit, but still standing. Its location protected the walls from the worst of the storms and wind. The roof sagged inwards, but it had not collapsed. Caliban had built it well. The ancient curtain had long since rotted from the doorway, leaving it open to travelers and island creatures alike. Yet Caliban knew instinctively, as he knew everything about the island, that he was the first to cross its threshold since Prospero had gone away.

IV.iv.

The sea currents pushed at her, twisted against the magic, then fell away. She trudged on, the silt of the sea bottom rising in small puffs with every step. The water was cold, even through the shield of her magic. She began to look only at her feet, because her eyes grew tired from peering into the gloom, and the sea creatures made her nervous. And so it was that she literally stumbled over the first of the cages.

It was bell-shaped, made of some strange silvery metal that was woven in crossed strips like a basket. She knocked it on its side with her foot, imagining it a piece of wreckage from a sunken ship. As it fell over, a bubble of light rose from beneath it. The bubble stretched and took on the ghostly shape of a man. It turned to face Chiara, its eyes wide and wild and burning. Then it fled upward, streaking away to the surface like a star falling through space.

Bewildered, Chiara looked around and saw more of the bell

shapes. The sea floor was littered with them. Now she noticed that every one contained a dull glow. She tipped another onto its side, gingerly. Again a ghostly man of light rose and sped away, but this one paused a moment to touch her cheek before racing to the surface. Its touch warmed her. Wonderingly, she put her own hand upon the spot and then looked at the palm, expecting to see some stain of the creature's light on her own skin.

That was how the mermaid found her, staring at her hand as though reading the map of her own destiny. She fell on Chiara like a fury, tearing at her face and clothes, her two rows of sharpened teeth biting through Chiara's protective magic. "Those are my souls, human. Mine!" she hissed.

They fought, wrestling with one another on the seabed. Her tail pummeled Chiara, her long dark hair wound around Chiara's neck like choking fronds of seaweed. Chiara struck back repeatedly, hitting in a wild and frenzied manner. She'd never fought anyone in her life, but now she bit and thrashed with desperation. In their struggle they knocked over several more of the metal cages. The freed souls swirled around them before rising to the surface. The mermaid pushed Chiara away from her and began to snatch at the fleeing spirits. Chiara had never seen such hatred and horror as she saw on the ghostly faces. She grabbed at the mermaid and shouted, "Let them go! They don't belong to you! Let them go!"

The mermaid turned on Chiara, her snake eyes alien and unblinking. "Of course they belong to me," she hissed. "I've gathered this field of souls for over four hundred years. I know every one as well as if it were my own. They are my own. They are mine! If you dare touch another I will rend your own pathetic half-soul from you, no matter what magic you have to protect yourself. Go away!"

Chiara shook her head to clear it. She wiped her hand across a small wound on her brow that leaked blood, dark and cloudy, into the water. A shark descended toward her, shying away from her magical shield, then veering back. She closed her eyes and breathed slowly, willing her cuts to heal. The bleeding stopped, and the shark drifted off once more in its endless pursuit of prey.

"I've done magic," Chiara said to herself, wonderingly. She could still feel the burn in her veins where it had passed on its healing course.

The mermaid sneered contemptuously. "Small magic," she said. "It will not be enough to save you."

Chiara rubbed her wrist, then self-consciously let her arms fall back to her sides. It was hard not to agree with the creature. "What do you mean, my 'half-soul'?" she asked. "I am human."

The mermaid laughed. "Do you think that's enough? You're only half grown, girling. You're incomplete. Life hasn't tested you yet." Her teeth showed, dagger sharp, framed by full, dark lips.

"Life is testing me as we speak," Chiara said. It seemed an obvious point.

"Well, go grow up then," the mermaid said. "And keep away from me and my cages, you hear? Otherwise I'll fit one for you."

Chiara stared at her. "Why do you want them?" she asked. She couldn't help herself. And chatting with a mermaid, even a wicked, violent mermaid, was better than what was waiting for her.

The mermaid tilted her head to one side and stared at her. "They are pretty," she replied with a shrug. "I like to have them. I like to hear them cry. They are the sound of the sea." Again her smile deepened, this time forming dimples in her cheeks.

Chiara thought again of the warmth of the departing soul's touch, of the horror the others showed when they caught sight of the mermaid. "They are meant to be free," she said. "You are a monster to them."

The mermaid shrugged her shoulders again, still cheerful in her brutality. "Every one of them gave himself to me. Every one threw himself to my waiting arms. It is not my fault that they dreamed of a warm maid on a sandy shore, and not a cold bed at the bottom of the sea."

"Of course it's your fault. You promise them love, lure them to their doom. Caliban has told me stories of you, singing with your sisters, in the days before my grandfather banished you from the shores of the island."

"Caliban," the mermaid hissed. "So you keep company with the moon-man. He is a traitor to all the wild. Tell him," she said, swimming closer, her eyes narrowing, "tell him that if he ever sets his foot in the waves, my sisters and I will rip his pitiful soul from him and chain it to the seabed for all eternity. Tell him that he will never see his star brothers again."

Chiara backed away. "He is not a traitor," she replied. "He didn't harm the island. He has vowed to heal it. You have no right to hate him."

"I have every right, mortal. Caliban was meant to be our king, and he left us all, wounded and dying. And for what? To serve Prospero in a foreign land."

"Caliban is a good man," Chiara argued. "And so was my grandfather."

"Prospero." The mermaid spat the name out, her eyes hard and glittering. "He was the enemy of all wild things. No magic could exist that would not serve him and his own purposes. No doubt Caliban has grown the same. He will never call the island home again. Tell him that, when next you see him."

Chiara stepped further back from her acidic, roiling hatred, but she did not turn away. "I've come for my grandfather's spell book," she said after a moment. "I need it for its power. Caliban and I are going to heal the island. You will have to bury your spite then, mermaid."

"You want the spellbook for its power to help us." The creature laughed mirthlessly. "So says every human when they first come to the wild. Soon help becomes control, and then control becomes possession. I know just how far to trust you, Prospero-girl."

"I wish people would stop calling me that. My name's Chiara. And I don't want to possess you, or even control you." She stopped. She had freed the souls, after all. "I don't like what you do," she went on. "Maybe I will stop you, if I can. But you are free to live here, beneath the waves…"

The mermaid stared at Chiara contemptuously. "You don't know anything about wild ways at all, human," she said at last. "Do you plan to just walk up to the Leviathan and ask for the book?"

Chiara imagined the monster's maw gaping wide, swallowing oceans and spewing hot sulfur across the seabed. Resolutely, she pushed away the thought. "He sleeps," she replied, with false confidence. "I will take it from him."

The mermaid's laughter floated in silvery bubbles around Chiara, snaring her. She swam around the girl, brushing Chiara with the cold scales of her tail, her translucent fins raising the fine hairs on her body. "He knows you are coming," she said, her voice low and singing. "You plod across the sea, human-born." She brought her face close to Chiara's. Her lips smiled, but Chiara winced at the carrion smell of her breath.

In the lulling of the mermaid's magic Chiara remembered lying beside a stream, trailing her hand in the icy waters until a fish swam into her palm. She remembered gently tickling the fish until it was in a stupor, then pulling it, gasping and floundering, onto the bank. And she remembered her horror when Caliban took it from her grasp and dashed its head against the rock. "It's quicker that way, Chiara," he'd said. "You wouldn't want it to suffer."

With a sudden wrench Chiara pushed away from the mermaid, somehow ducking the siren's power with her own magic. The mermaid shrieked in rage, her teeth gnashing, and her tail foaming the water. "I am not as witless as you think, lady," Chiara said, holding the creature at bay with newfound strength. The mermaid writhed and twisted, but Chiara sensed that she had given up on her prey. She knew Chiara was no longer helpless.

Chiara moved away from her and her ocean-field of souls. The mermaid watched, her hair wafting in the current. "You are going to your doom," she said. Chiara didn't reply. The mermaid bent and picked up one of the now-empty cages. "Don't worry," she called out, "I shall keep your soul safe with me. We shall have all of eternity together." She laughed, but the waters carried the sound away. The darkness of the deeps closed around her.

IV.v.

Caliban stood in the doorway and stared into the humble dwelling. There were the rough wooden beds on either side of the tiny cell. There was the equally rough table set between them, against the wall across from the doorway. There were the remnants of two chairs, as well, obviously made of some inferior wood because they lay broken on the floor on either side of the table. He rubbed his right hand, remembering the cut he'd given himself while building the furniture. It had seemed so alien to him. The table and chairs were odd enough, but why would anyone want to sleep on a wooden platform? He never did make a bed for himself. He slept in the corner on a pile of straw and boughs. *Like a mule*, he thought. Then he tossed the resentment away. Sleeping on the floor had been his preference, his choice.

He entered the hut and ran his hand across the table, sweeping aside the dust of one and a half decades. The surface of the table was stained and scratched. It was strange, now, to imagine Chiara's royal mother here, living in a place as mean as this.

Something was lying on the longer of the two beds. At first he thought that he had been mistaken, that some creature had come in here to die in comfort. He lifted what appeared to be a dead bird from the torn covers. Dust flew from the feathers, assailing his nose and memory at once. It wasn't a corpse he held.

"I want a cape, Caliban," Prospero had said, long ago, when Caliban still thought the old man was a god. "I need something to keep out the wind and weather, but fine, too, so it's worthy of my magic. Can you do it?"

He'd been so eager to prove his worth to Prospero. All these years later, even in the gloom of the cabin, the ancient cape he'd made from cormorant skins seemed to shine. Caliban held it for a moment, gazing down at the shimmering blue-black of the feathers; then, with a quick decisive gesture, he threw it around his shoulders. In that instant, he was the island king, here to claim his throne.

The moment passed quickly. He shook the cape from his shoulders and stood, stroking it. He remembered how he had caught them. It had been easy. They had trusted him. And he remembered how he had killed them and skinned them and eaten their flesh. His face twisted into a wry grimace. The birds had not tasted very good.

He stroked the feathers again. His work had been well done. He remembered curing the skins carefully, then sewing them together so that they poured over Prospero's back like black water. And he remembered watching while Prospero worked his magic into the garment, making it his own. Jeweled water, obsidian power.

"I was the tailor, not the prince," Caliban said aloud.

His glance strayed across the other bed, Miranda's bed. The first time her father had tucked her in there, she'd been so small, her blue eyes wide and fearful. "It's such a big bed, Father," she'd said. "And I'm such a little girl."

Prospero had sat beside her. "It won't always be so big," he told her. "You grow taller and stronger every day. Now close your eyes, and I'll tell you a story."

Caliban had sat there in the corner, watching the two of them. Prospero's story was about a princess who was so beautiful she made the goddess Venus jealous. The goddess had sent her son to kill the princess, but he fell in love with her and took her away to a secret castle, where he married her. But the princess was sad because her husband would only visit her at night, and she'd never seen his face. She finally lit a lamp one night and looked at him. He was so handsome her hand shook and she spilled oil on him. He awoke and was angry, and she had to do many tasks before he agreed to love her again. But she worked very hard, and so she was made into a goddess herself. It was Miranda's favorite story. She asked for it nearly every night.

It became his favorite as well. Perhaps, if he worked as hard as the princess, the wizard would love him.

He watched his memories for a long time, lulled by the pattering of rain on the roof. Finally, his mind recognized what his eyes saw on the bed. He froze. It was the staff, the wizard's staff, the power of the island broken in two. From the jagged edges bled the strength and health of the island. Here was the cause of the island's suffering. Tenderly he lifted it up, fitting the halves into each other and willing them to knit together. For a brief instant there was a check in the island's pain, but it resumed again.

He squatted down and laid the two pieces on the floor, once more pushing the two broken halves together. Then he grabbed at one of the decaying blankets and tore a strip from it. This length of cloth he wrapped around the break, pulling it tight. Caliban had always been clever with knots. And he had learned, without wanting to, some of the wizard's magic that would bind where nothing else would. Alone, he could not mend the staff. But he could fashion a bandage that would slow the draining of the island's life. He whispered the words of power into the tying. The old fabric strengthened. The knot almost slipped, then held fast.

In the very root of his soul he could feel the island rest.

He lay down on Prospero's old bed, the staff in his arms. He held it as though it were his beloved. "Forgive me," he whispered. "I did not know."

He felt no response.

The rain continued to slither down from the sky. He stared out the open door and recalled his last days here on the island. He remembered stumbling about drunkenly with two stranded sailors. One of the men he'd made his false god. The other was a court jester. "A cruel fool," he said out loud, as though he could chase away the memory with a silly rhyme. He remembered how the spirits of the island had tormented the three of them.

Well, he deserved it. He had betrayed everyone: island, Prospero, Miranda, spirits, the cormorants. There was a long list of suffering caused by his weakness and stupidity.

And now Chiara's name was added to that list.

The memories finally fell away, and he buried his face in his arm.

He should have torn up the handkerchief. He should never have given her this choice. What was marriage, and a foreign court, compared to being killed by a monster? What sort of father was he, to let his child meet such a fate?

What did it matter if the island died, so long as Chiara lived?

The thought was betrayal upon betrayal. He felt the island pull away from him. But he could not take it back. If he balanced Chiara against the island…

That was what he had done. That was what Chiara had done. He remembered her at age four, trying to thread a needle. They had been making kites. It was a windy autumn day, and Caliban was impatient to go outside. He kept reaching to help her, to hurry her along. "I want to do it myself, Caliban," she said. It took her almost half an hour to put that thread through the needle's eye. She cried, but she never gave up. And when it was done, she had smiled so proudly. "I shouldn't have doubted you," he'd said to her.

But he still did. He never learned. He even preferred it when she failed, when she turned to him for help. She was still his child.

And so he found the heart of his pain. It was not a foreign

prince or a dragon who would take Chiara from him. It was life itself. She would grow up, and he would fade in importance. He had tried to keep her, by bringing her here. But she was no longer his, and fate would not let him be so grasping. "She will be killed in the sea, or she will return a wizard, forever changed," he said aloud. His voice was raspy, the words sounding small and faint. But he knew they were true.

And which did he want? Did he truly want her to live, to emerge from the water a dragon-slaying wizard? She'd never need his help again.

If she died, she'd be his forever. He'd die, the island would die. They'd all slip away. He'd keep Chiara by losing her.

"I am a monster," he said. "I am a thing of darkness."

He lay there, the staff cradled loosely in his arm, and stared up at the sagging roof. He could think of nothing more contemptible than himself.

IV.vi.

Chiara went on, plodding around the decaying wrecks that sprawled and hulked in the cold and dark. She didn't question the direction she walked, certain that she was going straight to the great beast. Her steps faltered only when she felt herself drawing nearer. There was a sudden warmth in the dark water, a smell of sulfur, a pulse of phosphorescence that stretched an impossibly long distance. What did she intend to do?

"He knows you're coming," the mermaid had said. Were they just words to frighten her, or was she telling the truth?

The floor of the ocean became pebbled. She trod slowly over fist-sized stones, smooth and rounded by the sea. That was strange, so far out in the deeps, where she imagined there would be nothing but sand and silt.

And then the monster appeared before her, its inner fires fed by every beat of its volcanic heart. A new wave of heat engulfed Chiara, uncomfortably hot, even within her magical shield. By the strange red glow of the beast, she took in the sight of seven massive heads piled upon each other, like a demonic litter of puppies. *That's all wrong,* she thought to herself. It was the central head that held the monster's own tail within its jaws, loosely, almost delicately, though those hinges could clearly crush a boulder of granite and feel nothing in the effort.

One of the heads smelled her. It was instantly roused, lifting and turning its snakey eye to peer at her. "Chiara," it said, the giant black fork of its tongue tasting the waters as it spoke. "Come closer. I wish to see you more clearly."

There was no disobeying the command. She drew nearer. She did not question how the monster knew her, knew her name. Of course it did. It was the Oldest. Was there anything it did not know? The other heads opened their eyes and looked at her from every angle, one winding around behind her, its tongue flickering down the length of her back. Still, the central head slept on.

Images flashed through Chiara's mind: dizzying, giant storms of color. The heads were conferring with one another, speaking in the ancient way of the dragon. Chiara caught vague phrases. *It's like chatting with a thunderstorm,* she thought to herself. One of the heads stopped and spoke to her mind directly. It had a beard, and for a wild moment it reminded her of her grandfather. It was amused by her. "You are right," it said, in images that ripped across the chamber of her skull. "I wield the thunderball and bring the rains of spring."

"You're only supposed to have one head," she said to it. Idiotically, she knew, but she couldn't stop. "All the drawings of you show one head."

Cosmic laughter punctured her brain. The central head awoke, its heavy, leathery outer eyelids lifting, its inner membranous ones sliding away to the sides. The eyes of this head were golden-green and had round pupils, an owlish monstrosity. They caught her mind and held it prisoner, effortlessly tearing from her every thought and every secret desire she'd ever had. She was left with just enough thought to know that she was nothing at all.

The great jaws of the central head opened wide, a lazy yawn of terror. Chiara did not even bother to cover her face with her hands as it swallowed her whole.

Mercifully, she fainted.

Time passed, how much she did not know. All around her was black. Death-dark, grave-black. It was hot, wet, and impossible. Chiara lay on the oozing floor of the beast's body, waiting to die. She did not understand why she was not yet dead. How could a person be swallowed whole, and live?

"How, wizardling?" asked a cool serpentine voice in her mind. She sat upright, feeling the heavy weight of water and time, both slipping past and coiling around the great beast. She felt his bones and knew they were the bones of the earth. She was in the heart of the world.

"Not exactly the heart," said the great voice again, amused. "But I see how you think, small one. You may live. The power does lie within you. But you must find it first, and time, youngling, is not your friend."

"Power?" Chiara whispered. "I must fight my way out with magic?"

It seemed as though the very earth laughed at that. "Fight? Magic?" said Leviathan. "What strength can you have, human, that can compare with my own? Force will not free you, nor will tricks. Seek deeper, small one."

"Deeper, how? Deeper inside myself, or deeper in you?" She looked about wildly, then shut her eyes against the maddening darkness.

There was no answer. The Leviathan was finished talking with her. She could sense its mind: withdrawn, faintly curious.

What power did she have?

Her thoughts went to alchemy, of course. In the beginning she had studied it just to spend time with her grandfather. But his passion had become her own. "I am in the furnace now," she said aloud. "I am the lead." Sweat streamed over her. "And it won't be long until I've completely melted."

She waited for something to happen: a revelation, a sudden burst of knowledge. Nothing happened except that she became so hot she thought she could feel her skin crackle.

It was hopeless. Her mind would not work. She wasn't able to think. She fell back onto the soft, moist flesh of wherever she was. The dragon's gullet? Its belly? How long could she last in this place?

She began to cry. It was ridiculous, this death. Why should she care about this island? She had betrayed her father and risked the peace of two nations so that she could die alone at the bottom of the sea in the belly of a great beast.

It was so preposterous, her tears turned to laughter. There was no joy in it, just a maddened, hysterical, rib-wrenching convulsion that stretched on and on until she was left breathless and drained. She stretched out on her back. The position made her think of Caliban and of staring at the stars. "I wish I could see you now," she whispered.

She remembered the first time they had gone to the tower to watch the stars. He'd been stiff and formal because the queen had officially made him her teacher. She had wanted to tease him, to make him laugh and be her friend again, but because she loved him, she knew that would hurt him. His master's role hung about him like a poorly fitted cloak. So she was quiet and still and careful in her movements and speech. She'd been a bit shy, too, of course. She repeated everything he told her, committing it to memory. He was so wise, knew so much. She didn't want to seem a dunce.

But the times and positions of the stars had tangled in her mind. She had grown frustrated and flippant in their lessons. So Caliban told her the stories of the stars. His brothers, he called them. The heavens began to make sense. She learned the royal stars: Aldebaran, Rigel, Antares, Fomalhaut and Spica, all with their meanings and omens and portents.

Chiara repeated their names now, out loud, as though Caliban were here to praise her for learning them so well. In the dark they became familiar friends who could comfort her. But it was Sirius, the dogstar, she really loved. He was the first star she could recognize and remember. She admired his loyalty to Orion, the way he trotted across the heavens at the hunter's heel. Caliban loved him too, said that he was his closest brother, that they both had been born to serve.

Those words, unremarkable for so long, now jangled the chords of memory. Chiara frowned. The mermaid had said that Caliban was meant to be the island king. Her grandfather had kept him as a servant, instead. Chiara tried to imagine Caliban, who lived and walked in shadows and darkness, who bowed and toiled and kept his own council, as a king. He was nothing like her father, the King of Naples. Ferdinand was tall and strong and handsome. He strode in the sun, gave commands in a voice that echoed, demanded compliance. He moved at the center of his counselors, the axel in the wheel of state.

"He is sulfur to Caliban's mercury," she muttered.

Moon-calf, quicksilver; Caliban was a creature of the night. No wonder he saw the stars as his brothers. Her mind wandered back to the old memories.

"Are you out there, dogstar?" she said into the darkness.

IV.vii.

Two of the Leviathan's heads lifted and looked at one another. "That would be an interesting way out," one said.

"If she can do it," the other replied. "Humans find it hard enough to reach the stars when they're staring right at them."

"Hmm," said the first head. It had a small beard on its chin and a more kindly look to its eyes. "I hope she makes it."

"Small surprise," snorted the second head. This one had red eyes in its black, dog-like face. It had a double row of teeth in its mouth, all of them sharpened like razors. "You always did have a soft spot for the wretched mortals."

"They are our children, too," the first head chided.

"Be quiet," grumbled a third head with a horsey look to its countenance, complete with small pointed ears, long snout, and square teeth. "She mustn't hear us speak anymore. We'll spoil the trial."

All the heads settled down upon one another, eyes drifting

shut. But the first head stayed awake, listening to the struggle within.

It had always had a soft spot for the humans, after all.

⌒⋉

He was the brightest star in their small sky. His rise heralded their lazy days of summer; the "dogdays," after their foolish name for him. It amused him that this was how they saw him, those quick pale flashes of thought that flickered and fought and died so far from him. They did not even count him among their great stars, he who burned with a light more than twenty times that of their own little yellow sun.

It did not bother him. He knew his own greatness. It pleased him when one of the small ones reached out to him.

He could hear her calling him, seeking him out in the great expanse. It was the one his small brother loved. She was blind and distant, muffled somehow. She had talked to him for many years now, and he always replied, but she never listened. She had never tried to hear him before.

He could sense that she was trying to hear him now.

⌒⋉

The darkness pressed against her face, but Chiara forced herself to stare through it, to let her mind travel out into the high heavens. "I am lost," she whispered. "Dogstar, can you help me? Can you show me the way home?"

There, alone in the belly of the beast, Chiara saw the heavens spinning like a great wheel, spraying out fountains of light and life. The starry host danced its turning through the ages. Time ran around the clock, seasons around the year.

And Leviathan circled the world, his tail caught between his jaws.

"What does it mean?" wondered Chiara.

All journeys lead back to their beginning, the heavens hummed.

"What's the sense of that?" Chiara said. "If you just end up where you started then nothing changes."

You change. And that changes everything.

"So what am I to do? Wander the length of Leviathan until I end up back in his jaws?"

Small thinking will not save you.

"What will save me, then?" Chiara cried.

You must find the path within yourself and follow it.

"What path?"

The path that leads you where you've most wanted to go. Find the way, small one.

The light spun in her mind, illuminating the desires of long ago, buried in the depths of memory. She was five, dancing in the palace garden with Caliban watching her, laughing. She was older, maybe seven, sitting in a carriage with her mother and wearing an impossibly stiff gown. The carriage slowed, and a small group of Romani children raced by, laughing, talking their wild, freewheeling speech. She was ten, and Caliban was show-ing her the skeleton of a dead gull. She remembered tracing the bones of the wings with her finger, wishing that these were her arms, that she could fly high and free. She was twelve, and had finally been permitted to read from the books in the castle's great library. She read all that she could find about Marco Polo and his travels, dreamed of walking the treacherous Silk Road herself.

Good.

Good? What did these memories do for her? The light pulsed through her brain. "I want to be free," she said.

There were fountains, laughter, music in her mind.

Go then, small one. Be free.

The dark descended again, rolling through her mind. But it had lost its power to smother. She flipped over onto her belly, pulled up her skirt, and knotted it around her waist. On all fours, like a baby and with a baby's determination, she began to crawl. "This is the way out," she said, with gritted teeth. "All ways are the way out, if I have the patience. That must be the answer."

And she crawled. Time stretched out, the darkness went on, and still she crawled. She crawled for hours, crawled until her mind became as numb as her limbs. Then she slept, deep within the belly of the dragon. When she awoke she felt calm, as though her life were behind her, as though it were only a story she'd heard once long ago when she was a child.

Her crawling had not brought her any closer to freedom. It had been a ridiculous idea. Well, at least it had drained her fear away. Her troubles would soon be over, she was sure of it. There were moments when she could feel the weight of the world pressing down upon her. Her shield of magic was failing.

She would fail. Her soul would be taken by that hateful

mermaid. The island would die. Caliban would die, alone, with the world slipping into decay around him.

It was that thought of him, of his pain and despair, that threw her back into life. She sat up, her legs tucked under her, her back straight, her hands resting loosely on her knees. This was how Caliban used to sit when he was thinking through an alchemical problem for her grandfather. He kept a small mat in a corner of his workroom where he would meditate his way through their next course of action. She'd gone looking for him there many times and had turned away when she saw him sitting, his gaze unfocused. He never responded when he was in that state.

The memory was painful. It brought back the sound of her grandfather's voice calling instructions from his chair; the smell of the herbs in the backroom; the feeling of the sunshine streaming in through the window, warming the table where Caliban did his work. Home.

She swallowed her tears and tried to remember what Caliban had told her about his meditation. He said that he would sit until everything grew still in his mind. Once he found that peace, then the answer he was seeking would be revealed. The results from these sessions had never impressed her. But the spell was growing thin around her. It was better to die while trying something.

It did not take long before she was chewing her nails in frustration. She'd always supposed that it would be easy to not think. It would be as simple as not moving. But her mind was full of noise and confusion. The more she tried to be still, the more her thoughts raged.

She hit the floor of her prison with her hands until they

stung, cursing the beast as she did so. When she grew tired she sat back again. Her breathing slowed. She grew calm once more. She thought of nothing.

She did not notice when the shield fell.

⌒

"Temperamental creature," remarked the horse head. "I don't think much of all that flailing."

A green and purple scaled head lifted. It was the snakiest of them all, smooth and beautiful and deadly. It hissed in agreement. "Humans," it said, "know nothing of patience. It comes from that warm blood of theirs. They can't sit still. They don't know how to wait."

"It makes them tasty, though," said the dog-like head, its eyes glowing sulfurously.

The horse head snorted in laughter.

The bearded head frowned. Gently it nuzzled at the book between their paws. A large head, armored with plates and horns, watched with interest. "You will be happy to give it to her," it said.

The bearded one startled, then relaxed. They were similar, these two, in their interest in the younger creatures of the Earth. It was true that this other cared for the humans only because they mined the ground for the gold it loved so dearly. But it would not taunt him like some of the others.

"The island must be healed," it replied. "We all agree to that."

Something shifted. All the heads rose as one, tasting the change. "There is another," the snake head hissed. "Do you feel her? She slips the bonds of magic even now."

"This should be interesting," the armored head said.

IV.viii.

The ship rested in the harbor, held fast in the chains of a spell that kept all the souls aboard asleep and content. Dreams were spun and woven for each one. A smile caressed every face.

Every face but one. Calypso, orphaned child of a Greek mother and a Turkish father and at home in no land, slipped loose from the knots of magic and awoke.

The silence of the ship made Calypso's skin prickle with fear. She gazed around at her slumbering comrades laid out upon the deck boards in a peaceful mock death. Rising, she moved swiftly among them, assuring herself that they were alive. She had been a sailor for two years now, could scarcely remember what it was like to sleep alone in a room of her own. The snores and grunts and mumbled phrases of the others were so familiar that she only noticed them now that they were gone. She was happy to quit their silent company and go out on deck.

The fog had lifted, but a steady grey drizzle fell. It crept under the collar of her shirt and turned her hair to wet wool. Calypso sensed that it was early morning. There was no telltale sun hovering low in the sky, but she knew the smell of daybreak.

She was thin, crafty with her hands, and she seldom spoke. Her eyes were dark and heavy lidded. People always said she looked as though she was hiding a secret. They were right. Her features were even, her skin smooth, but something about her face was neither male nor female. She was the ship's boy.

The island before her now was a dreary land; that much Calypso could see. But it beckoned to her. Its strangeness spoke to her in a way that no land ever had before. She had left Greece when she was eleven, after she was orphaned. She had not grieved. Her parents had done their best with her, but she grew up knowing that she was an intruder, that she had upset the cheerful rhythm of their life together. The notion hadn't bothered her. It didn't matter that she was just a visitor in their home. Her fate was somewhere far away. With their deaths, she had run to meet it. She had made herself a boy and gone to sea.

But her ruse could not continue. She was thirteen now, and womanhood was upon her. The small magic of illusion she wore had grown thin. Her body was still lean and muscled, but there was a new softness about her face where a boy should have the early shadowings of a beard. Her body was betraying her. She had started to feel suspicious eyes following her around the ship.

The storm had saved her. They had fought against the wind and waves for three days, resting in short shifts, often not sleeping at all. No one had had a moment to stare at her, to wonder aloud to his crew mate. They had simply shouted orders and relied on her skills to help save them all. In the fury of the storm, she was their brother once again.

Well, she was not their brother. And now this strange island offered her an escape. The dismal shore before her called out to something in her blood. Calypso stared at it nervously, the long fingers of her right hand raking the dark hair that hung in ragged chunks to her shoulders. Oddly, she was struck with the memory of watching her mother brushing her hair in the sunlight. She hadn't brushed her own hair in years. When it got too long, one of the other sailors cut it for her with his knife.

She let her hand drop and considered her options. She knew how to swim. It was rare among sailors, but she had never had a fear of the water. She'd splashed in it since she was a small child. Often she would spend the day out on the water with old Nick, one of the fishermen. He had no children of his own and was grateful for her help. "I don't care if you're a girl, so long as you can pull in a net," he used to growl. She would often jump from the boat to play with the dolphins in the sea. There was one that seemed to be her friend, to seek her out on fine days. Nick said it brought them luck. Truthfully, leaving Nick had been her only sadness. He'd have trouble with his nets without her. She had used his name as her own. He'd like that, she guessed.

Now she leapt into the sea once again. She had never been one to hold back.

The water was colder then she expected and seemed to pull at her. Calypso struggled her way to the shore, thrashing against unusual currents. Finally, she pulled herself up onto a stony beach and lay down for a moment on the pebbles, staring up at the leaden sky. She let the spitting rain wash the salt from her face.

At last she got up and began to search about, exploring her new world. She headed inland, toward the trees. Something was calling to her. She walked as though she knew where she was going. Everything was foreign, but also familiar. It felt as though she was in a place she'd once dreamed about. She couldn't remember any such dream. But when she grabbed a branch that had snagged itself on her hair, she was sure that she'd brushed it away before, just like this, in this place.

"I know it all," Calypso said. Then she shook her head, because she didn't understand what her own words meant. She just felt they were true, and she followed a path she knew but didn't know until she found what was calling her.

There was an abandoned shack in the clearing, its door open. She made straight for it, praying that its roof was intact. Something about the rain bothered her. As a sailor, she had come to know all the temperaments of weather. This drizzle reeked of magic, strong magic. She was happy to be out of it.

Calypso stood in the center of the hut, dripping water onto the dirt floor, and looked around at the humble furniture. Something was wrong here, too. She had the sense that someone had been here only recently. The covers on one of the beds were rumpled. "Probably an animal," she said aloud. Her voice sounded harsh and grating. It seemed to violate the lonely house. Instantly she knew she was wrong. No animal would shelter here. This was an unhappy place.

And now she could see why. There was a staff lying on the bed. It was bound around the middle. She knew why. She could feel it oozing power. Her fingers prickled as she reached for it. "This is why I have come here," Calypso whispered. It seemed to her that there was nothing in the world she wanted so much as the staff. "You are mine," she said. But as soon as her hand touched the wood she felt a burning jolt. She pulled away at once. Whatever power it was didn't want her. She began to shiver.

"It doesn't like you," said a voice.

Calypso spun around, and then stepped back further in the room when she saw the fiery creature in the doorway. "Are you a demon?" she croaked. It laughed then, showing a mouth full of flickering flames. Then it seemed to steady and become iridescent, a creature of light rather than fire. "Hardly," it said, speaking her native Greek as effortlessly as herself. "I'm a spirit of the air. I am called Ariel."

"Calypso," she replied. The simple act of saying her name made her laugh. For the past two years she'd called herself Nikos. The last of her disguise fell, making her suddenly awkward. She wrapped her arms around herself, for protection. *I don't remember how to be a girl,* she thought. She almost tried to weave the spell again. But she didn't.

They watched each other warily, curiously. Finally Calypso asked, "Do you live here?"

Ariel laughed. "I live nowhere and everywhere. This hut belonged to the island king, before he left us. I expect Caliban will go back to his cave."

"Caliban?" she said, repeating the funny name.

"He has come back to the island," Ariel explained. "He arrived yesterday, with your ship."

Of course. The male passenger, the strange, spotted man in the hood who had called her Hermes. She had smelled the magic in him, and in the young princess too, when they had come aboard. "So, he was the reason for the storm? And for the spell on the ship? He is the king of this place?" she asked.

The spirit smiled, his purple eyes unreadable. "After a fashion," he said.

"I don't understand," Calypso said, irritation making her voice sharp.

"Yes," the spirit said, "Caliban caused the storm. But he is not the king." He sneered contemptuously.

She looked back at the bed. "And this staff, the broken one that doesn't like me, is this his as well?"

"Not really," the spirit replied. He looked wary. He didn't trust her.

"Where is this Caliban?" she asked.

"He's gone to the shore again. To wait."

Calypso decided that she had had enough of riddles. She turned back to the staff lying on the bed and grabbed it around the cloth bandage, gasping as she lifted it upright. The power of it shot through her, making the fine hairs on her arms stand straight. She held on, tasting the magic. It seared her hand, but she ignored the pain.

The whole island was there, in the staff. She could feel its weakening pulse, followed it out to the wild wizard huddled on the shore. He, in turn, was tied to a thread of life that stretched out into the deeps of the sea, beyond the staff's reach. The princess, gone below the waves. The island waited for her return.

The pain in Calypso's hand made her drop the staff back onto the bed. She stood staring at it, rubbing her sore hand against her thigh as she considered what she had seen. "It is a great wound," Ariel said, behind her.

She faced him again, holding her expression neutral, her voice steady. She had no map to follow the path to her desire. This spirit was tied to the island; and the island did not want her. But he was gazing at her hopefully. He wanted something from her. She might be able to use him.

"It is a great wound," she agreed. She looked back at the staff. "Can it be fixed?"

"Yes," said Ariel. "But it requires many powers, many magics, working together."

She traced the line into the sea once more, following it with her mind until it faded again. The princess had gone in search of new power. They would use it to mend the staff. And then Calypso would be cut off from it, and from everything it offered.

She could not go back to the ship. But she didn't want to live here as a servant, nothing but one more creature crawling across these rocks. Fate had not brought her to this place to let her rot on the shore. This island was hers. "I can help," she said. She spoke slowly and peered at the spirit from beneath the shadow of her eyelids.

"Good," the spirit said. Then he disappeared.

Calypso stood there for a moment, waiting to see if he'd return. Then she went to the doorway and looked around. Even on the dead ground, she could see the traces of an ancient fire pit. That would be welcome. Her clothes clung to her and the chill seemed to have become permanently lodged in her bones. She glanced up at the sky. The clouds were thick, unmoving. There would be no fire. She went back into the cabin, stripped off her wet clothes and sat on the other bed, wrapping herself in the ancient blanket. She was hungry, but that could wait. Even if the rain did not stop, she supposed this Caliban would bring something to eat when he came back.

Because he would come back for the staff.

She sat and stared at it. It seemed to whisper promises to her. "You will wield my power," the staff said. "You will be queen of the island, ruler over all the small lives."

She would be safe here. The angry sailors could not harm her. The memory of their faces blurred with those of the people of her village. They had thrown rocks at her and called her "witch-brat." They wouldn't dare throw anything if she had the staff. They'd be sorry for all the cruel things they'd done to her. They'd have to bow to her.

Calypso shook her head. Her hunger was making her confused. The people of her village would never see her. She didn't want to go back there. The island was enough for her. She didn't need anyone else.

Of course, there was this Caliban to contend with. Ariel suggested that he would be staying on the island, in "his cave." But that didn't seem likely. He and the princess were too fine to stay here. Probably they wanted to take the power with them to Spain, to help them rule.

Calypso shrugged her shoulders deeper under the thin blanket. Maybe the island didn't want her now, but it would learn to be grateful to her. She would keep the power here. She would take care of everything.

Calypso chewed at her lips. The others would insist on working the spell together. Well, she would find a way to help. And in the helping, she would bind the staff to herself.

She knew how to do such things. She was a witch-brat, after all.

IV.ix.

The rain still hissed and slivered down the sky, but Caliban was protected now by the cormorant cape. He had shaken off the sense of borrowed glory. The cape was simply practical. It would shelter him when he sat on the rocks. Ariel would not keep him away.

He had traveled quickly in the light of day. Walking and the warmth of the cape made him limber. He found some wild mushrooms on his way to the shore and ate them eagerly. He had missed the taste of island food. Soon he was back on the spit of land, once more hunched against the cold. The sea was quiet. Small waves softly undulated, merely licking at the land before they retreated. It looked and moved like liquid lead. He could not believe he had let Chiara go down into it. No one could survive under there. Not even his mother would have done it. He had stood by while Ariel spelled his girl into her grave.

"One crow sorrow," mocked a voice on his left.

He turned his head and glared at the spirit. Ariel smirked, his airy form unaffected by the weather he had brought down.

"They're cormorant feathers, not crow. As you know perfectly well," Caliban answered.

The spirit shrugged. "Small difference," he said. "You're still the picture of grief. Have you given up, then? The time is nearly past."

"But it is not, not yet." His words were hollow to his own ears. He had given up. But it did not matter anymore. He would die with the island. He would die with Chiara.

He felt suddenly peaceful. Staring into the alien eyes of Ariel he said, simply, "I am not my mother."

There was a pause. Ariel seemed to flicker. "I am not a rock," he said at last.

Caliban flapped his hand dismissively, a gesture learned from Prospero. "You know what I mean," he said.

"Do I?" Ariel replied.

"I never trapped you in the pine, Ariel. I had no power to stop my mother, nor any way to save you."

Ariel seemed to flame brighter. "Liar. Coward. After Sycorax died, you could have taken the staff. You would have been master. It would have been a simple matter to cleave the tree and free me. Instead, you gave the power to Prospero. You enslaved us all to his will, and then stood by as he broke the land and left it bleeding."

"So you keep saying," Caliban answered wearily. "But I remember, Ariel, how all those years you served Prospero willingly, even gratefully. And all that time, and even now, you never once thought to ask me why I did not use the staff."

"Because you are base born and stupid," Ariel snapped, "an earth-fool, made to serve."

The words were designed to wound. Once they would have sent him into a frothing rage, screaming that Setebos, his divine father, would strike and burn the spirit.

Now they just made him tired.

"I did not want to die the way my mother had died," he said, softly. "I hated the power she held. I hated what the staff made her become. I didn't want any of it. And I was a child when Prospero came to the island. He seemed like a god to me, then. I thought he would be wise, and kind, as king. And so he was," Caliban added, "in his own way. In the manner of other earthly kings."

Silence stretched out. Ariel flickered uncertainly. At last his light strengthened. "Well, it is past," he said, almost gruffly. For a moment he seemed almost mortal and contrite. "And it is not the reason I came to speak with you. We can do the healing now."

Caliban stared at him. "But the wizard's power? Chiara? You mean she didn't have to go beneath—" Anger made him choke. He rose, searching his mind for a way to injure the spirit.

Ariel flew higher, beyond him. "I didn't know, at the time. She was asleep. I couldn't sense her. She was caught in the spell."

"Who? Chiara? Chiara was with me the whole time, she was never—"

"Not the Prospero-girl," Ariel interrupted. "The other wizard girl, one who is familiar with her power. She is awake, and she has been to the hut, has held the staff. She says she will help us. Now."

Caliban staggered back. Another wizard, another girl? There had been another girl on the ship? "And Chiara?" he asked.

"She must fight her way back. That cannot be changed. She is far in the deeps, beyond our reach. But the island can be helped right now. Come."

Caliban shook his head. He felt witless and slow. Rain blurred his eyes. He wiped them with the back of his hand. His birthmarked, aging, useless hand, which could not save his child.

"What sort of girl is she?" he asked.

"What does it matter?" Ariel snapped. "She has none of Prospero's blood, at least. She will help us. Now come."

"But Chiara…" Caliban argued, clinging to his place on the rock. He would not break faith with her. He would not leave.

Ariel stopped. His eyes narrowed. "The island has been suffering for over sixteen years."

"Then it can wait two more hours," Caliban answered. Ariel flared, but Caliban pressed on. "If Chiara fails, then this new girl will do. But I will not let her go down into the deeps for nothing."

Ariel shrugged. "If she lives, she'll be a wizard. That should be enough for her."

Caliban gritted his teeth, but kept his reason. "Do you want to repeat my mistake? Do you really want to place the island in the hands of some unknown girl? I can vouch for Chiara. She will heal the island, not enslave it. Can this stranger be trusted?"

Ariel wavered. "Your hope is foolish. But we'll do it. We'll wait two more hours. We'll wait to the end of the spell, but no longer. When the Prospero-girl does not return, we'll do the healing with this other wizard. And if the Prospero-girl does survive...." He paused, and burned with a malignant glare. "If she does survive, then we'll use the better of the two."

Before Caliban could say a word the spirit vanished. He sat back down upon the rocks, his fears, impossibly, even greater. He wished he had not left the staff back at the hut. It had seemed safe enough at the time. But now some strange wizard girl was holding it, tasting its power. He shivered.

The rain continued to fall. Some time passed, perhaps an hour. And then, without warning, there was no time left.

He felt the thread of magic break. The shock of it raced through him, like a brand on his soul. He fell forwards and lay prone upon the rocks. Every joint in his body wrenched in protest. Chiara was gone. No matter how he tried, he could not sense her. It was over.

He stared at the sea with empty eyes. His heart slowed and turned to stone. He reminded himself, brutally, of every time she had told him of her nightmare of smothering beneath the weight of water. "Hush," he had said. "It will never happen."

He had let it happen.

Act Five

All That Glitters

V.i.

His stomach rumbled. It was ridiculous. Chiara was his life. How could he be hungry? Chiara would never be hungry again. Her face would never twist into its lopsided smile. It would bloat, and small watery creeping things would feast on her flesh. She would not even have a gravestone. He had called Ferdinand a fiend and a wretch for sending her away to be married. What was he then? He had sent her to her death.

He thought of following her under the waves. But the island still held him. Would he let Chiara die for nothing? Caliban looked back at the wet desolation of his first home. He couldn't leave this trail of misery behind him.

"I kill everyone and everything I love," he said. "I am Death."

He imagined how Chiara would laugh at him. She'd cheer, and say something like, "Bravo! That's the best piece of self-pity I've ever heard!"

But she wouldn't laugh. Or cheer. She was dead.

Caliban's mind winced and turned away from its own thoughts. He'd finish the work. The island would be healed. And then he would go to join Chiara.

In the meantime, he needed to be strong. He needed food. His old trout stream was nearby. He would try his luck. The stupid, idle phrase stabbed him. His luck. Caliban rose and walked away.

Scrambling through the loose bracken was hard. He got lost a number of times, and he cursed his clumsiness. "Prospero wouldn't need to use spirits to bedevil me now," he muttered. "I don't have the skill of a child." The knife of pain in his heart twisted again. He sat down on a lightning-scarred stump. Why should he save this cursed place? Let it die, and its evil power with it.

Grimly he stood and fought on through the underbrush. "I will not think these things," he muttered. "I am here, and Chiara is dead. I will do what I must do, and then I will rest. There is no other path." He kept repeating the words as he stumbled through the trees. They wiped away every other thought.

At last he found the stream. It was smaller than he remembered, and it took him nearly an hour to catch five fish, but time no longer held any meaning for him. He ran a straight stick through their gills and began to walk to his cave. He wasn't ready to face the new wizard yet.

His cave. It was unchanged and yet completely different. It was gloomier, and smelled moldy. The bed of boughs was still there. The branches had become hard and brittle. All the needles had fallen on the floor. He should burn it, along with the wood that he had left piled for that purpose. He had always made sure that there was wood for a fire. New boughs would have to be fetched for sleeping. He checked his thoughts. He wouldn't need a new bed.

He made the fire and cooked the fish, filled with a quiet peace. This cave had been his home and his haven, back in the days when he'd believed it was possible to be safe. Echoes of that feeling stirred in him, but they did not last. There was a strange wizard for him to meet.

A girl wizard.

Caliban gathered up the two remaining cooked trout. It was time. As he walked back to the hut, his only hope was that the girl would be nothing like Chiara.

But how could she be? There never had been anyone like her.

~

Calypso was shaken awake by a rough hand. She sat upright, pulling the blanket around her. Her clothes were still laid out on the floor, drying. Why had she fallen asleep? She'd slept long and deeply on the ship.

But all other thoughts vanished once she saw the man who awakened her. He was short, no taller than herself, and she was not yet fully grown. But he was broad and thick-muscled. His eyes were pale, ghostly, almost like a drowned man's. His hair was thin and fine and cinnamon-colored. It stuck up in odd tufts around his head, reminding her somehow of a newborn chicken. A very strange chicken. He was dressed in a long cape of black feathers. He looked like a giant portent of doom. She understood why he had kept himself covered with a hood on the ship. Instinctively she drew away from him.

He stepped back. "I won't harm you," he said.

She understood Italian well, but it formed awkwardly on her lips. "Thank you," she replied, and then blushed, because she knew how peculiar she sounded. She hated being ridiculous.

"My name is Caliban," he said slowly, hearing her foreign accent.

"This I know," she said. His eyebrows rose in surprise. "Ariel said this to me," she added.

"Ah, Ariel," he said. His face grew blank for a moment. "What else did he tell you?"

She chose her words carefully. She needed to be trusted. "That you have want for magic, for me helping a spell. I will do this."

Now that her mind was awake, she suddenly realized that he was alone. The princess was not with him. She felt a surge of hope, and then fought to keep it from her face. Even if he needed her, she would still have to be careful.

He nodded, his face still expressionless. "Good," he said. "What is your name, young wizard?"

Wizard. It was not a word she knew.

"Or should I just keep calling you Hermes?" he added. He smiled, and she felt suddenly that she trusted him.

"Near to this," she grinned. "My name, it is Calypso."

"So, a nymph, not a god," he teased.

Calypso felt her cheeks grow strangely hot. Life would be easier if she were Hermes, if she were a boy.

"But you are Greek," Caliban continued, half to himself.

"My mother, yes. My father, his is Turk."

"Ah. And you, Calypso, what are you?"

The question caught her off guard. He was clever, this ugly-looking man. She would have to be very careful. "I was sailor," she said, at last. "No more, now. This, ah, disguise, it never works, now. I am too old."

"Hmm," he replied. "Are you twelve, then?"

"Thirteen," she answered. She wished, desperately, that she had not taken off her clothes.

"That's a hard age, especially for a girl. I remember—" He broke off whatever he was going to say and covered his face with his hand for a moment. Calypso watched him warily.

He seemed to collect his thoughts. "This island has always been home to the homeless." His mouth twisted again, as though he had tasted something sour. "As long as they're magical," he added.

"You live here one time, before? You were, maybe, a ship-wreck here?"

He smiled again. It was a gentle smile. It reassured her. "I was born here," he said.

"Born?" She was confused. He could not mean what she thought.

"My mother was sent here, exiled, punished for being a witch. I was born here. We lived alone together, and then I lived by myself, for a while." He stopped.

"Oh," she said. A sudden rush of relief filled her. He wasn't a great royal man after all. "This I know, yes. For me, too, my mother was called this thing, 'witch.' With this, people, they are," she searched for the word, "cruel, yes?"

"Yes, cruel," he agreed. He lifted the leaf-wrapped bundle he had in his hand. "Fish," he said. "It's cooked. Are you hungry?"

She began to stretch out her arm, and then she remembered that she was still naked. "My cloths..." she stammered.

He blushed as well, his skin mottling an unusual purplish color. "I'll just leave this here, then, and fetch some wood. You'll want a fire."

He disappeared out the door. It was still raining. He'd have to let the wood dry in the hut for a time. He should have done that sooner. He'd build Calypso a shelter beside her fire, as well.

He thought of her eager dark eyes and how thin her shoulders were. No one had taken care of her for a long time. He wondered what would happen to her once the healing spell was done. She would have to stay on the island. It would be lonely for her. He would have to remember to tell her that.

"Here's a familiar sight," Ariel said, appearing in a tree above him. The spirit glowed and flickered in the boughs of the tree, turning the branches around him blue and gold. He made the day around him appear even more dismal.

Caliban glanced up at him. "My own burning bush," he said. He might have laughed at his own joke, if there had been any laughter left in him. Instead, he straightened his back, wincing as he did so. "It's a chore I loathe as much as ever," he replied, gathering all the wood into a bundle. He'd found a tree blown down, weathered enough to break up, not so old that it had begun to rot. It would have been a happy find, once.

"Do you suppose you could end the rain now, or are we not yet sufficiently dreary?" he asked. His joints pained him fiercely.

Ariel shrugged, then clapped his hands together. The rain immediately slowed, then ceased. In the sky, the clouds lifted enough to lighten the gloom. There was still no sign of the sun, but Caliban supposed that would come with the healing. "Thank you," he said. He managed to keep his tone civil.

"So, you've met the girl, then. What do you think?"

Caliban glared at him. "Were you there, watching?"

The spirit merely smiled in response.

Caliban shrugged angrily, but held on to his temper. "Then you'll know that all I've learned of her is that she's barely out of childhood and that she's been living as a sailor. Now make yourself useful and get this wood back to the hut."

They stared each other down, neither giving way until Ariel disappeared with an angry snort, the wood vanishing with him.

Caliban sat down on the stump of the tree and drew his cape in close around him. Ariel's question had been a fair one. What did he think of Calypso?

She was young, so young, but in many ways she seemed much older than Chiara. His heart stabbed in a painful sideways beat. "Don't compare them," he told himself. He said it out loud, to give it strength.

Calypso. Think of Calypso. What would make a girl disguise herself as a boy and run away to sea? She must be fearless. She was the sort of girl Chiara dreamed of being. Chiara had loved stories of bold, adventurous girls. She'd sit beside him in the evening and stare out the window as he spoke....

He stood. What did it matter what Calypso was like? She was strong enough, that was clear. She'd been working magic for years now. She seemed willing enough to help them.

He paused. Why had Ariel asked the question? He had already met the girl. Why didn't he just demand that they begin the spell at once? Something about the girl must bother him.

Caliban shrugged. Of course Ariel was suspicious of her. He hated wizards. But she was only a child. Surely he and Ariel could control her, even if she did turn out to be the most evil witch in the world. He thought of her stammering words and smiled. She was just a little lost soul.

And she needed a home. Perhaps, after the healing, he could stay with her for a while. Just to make sure that she was safe and happy. The island could be such a gentle place.

He began to walk back to the hut. Calypso wanted that fire. And as he walked he chewed back tears, because Chiara would never want a fire again.

V.ii.

Calypso leapt from the bed as soon as Caliban left. She pulled on her clothes. They were still unpleasantly damp, but she was used to that after living at sea. Then she snatched up the fish and ate it ravenously. It dented her hunger, at any rate. She longed for some bread.

Next she turned her attention back to the staff. She was not eager to touch it again, but she wanted to know more about its nature. Steeling herself against the onslaught of pain, she gripped the staff once more and sought out the knowledge she needed.

It told her of the days when it had roots, when it was nourished by earth and air, when it lived. Now it was a captured thing, trapped inside its own broken corpse. And it was she who did this.

She blinked and dropped the staff. Her palm was blistered from holding it. This made no sense. She hadn't been born when the staff was made. Yet it hated her, blamed her for the tree's death. It was absurd.

She would have to hide this from the others.

Calypso shook herself calm and went outside to fix up the ancient fire pit. She was absorbed in this task when a pile of wood suddenly materialized beside her. She jumped back, tripping over a stone and falling to the ground. "Sorry," said Ariel, appearing in the air before her. Suddenly she was back on her feet, dizzy and breathless.

"Stop it," she snapped. "I can take care of myself."

"Of course," he replied. "I was merely trying to help."

She bit her tongue. Let him think that she was meek. Let him think that he could control her. He was strong. She would need to surprise him to overwhelm his power.

"I thought Caliban was bringing the wood," she said.

"He found it," the spirit said. "He should be back soon. And then we can do the healing."

"But the princess? She is not coming back?" She hoped her voice was calm, neutral. She did not want to seem too eager.

Ariel shrugged. "She is gone," he replied, carelessly. "You will have to stand in her place as the wizard's power."

It was what she hoped for, but she still shivered at the thought of the drowned princess. Calypso loved the sea, but she wanted to die on land. Every sailor did.

But she would have known the risk, Calypso thought. And she still thought the power was worth it.

"How do we perform the healing?" she asked.

"We must stand at points and place the staff on the ground,

in the middle. Then we shall mend it, each in our own way, all at once. Do you know how to do it?" He looked suddenly afraid.

"Yes," she said. "It is a common spell."

The spirit looked at her sharply. She made herself stammer, as though confused. "I, I mean, is it like when you heal a bone? Or mend a broken pot?"

Now the spirit seemed worried. "Like that, I suppose," he replied. "Like both of them together. Do you think you can do that?"

"I think so, yes. I am good at such things," she said. She wanted to assure him of her ability and at the same time shield her strength. It was an awkward balance.

But she seemed to have achieved it because the spirit nodded in relief and began looking around. "We shall do it here, then," Ariel said, "Once Caliban returns." He looked impatiently at the trees. The agony of his waiting was palpable.

Silence stretched out between them. Calypso tried to make the fire, but she was awkward about it. It had been a long time since she'd had to do something like this. Finally she used a quick spell. It was an easy magic. Ariel barely glanced at her when it was done. Calypso sat back on a rock and let the new warmth calm her.

At last Caliban appeared, walking slowly from the shadow of the trees. He looked old and beaten. He would not be much of a threat. Then, as he came nearer, she saw his eyes. They looked like the eyes of her mother after her father's death. So, Caliban had loved the princess. She was sorry for him, but relieved as well. He did not look like he wanted the power for himself.

"Are you fit for the healing?" Ariel asked.

"Yes," Caliban replied. He glared at the spirit. "I will not fail."

"Good," Ariel replied. He glowed purple, his excitement obvious. "Let's begin," he said.

Caliban turned and went into the hut to fetch the staff. Calypso knew the instant he lifted it from the bed. She felt it pull away from her, but waiver. It was not sure that it wanted him, either. Better and better.

Caliban was clearly puzzled when he returned.

"What's the matter?" Ariel snapped at him. The spirit seemed to flicker impatiently.

"My connection to the staff," Caliban explained. "It's different. It seems... muffled...or muted."

"Everything is growing weaker. Hurry up," Ariel said.

Calypso said nothing. She tried to look faintly curious but disinterested. But neither of them looked at her. Their attention was only on the staff.

Caliban laid the staff on the ground. Gently he untied the knot in the bandage and pulled it away. The wound bled afresh, causing all three of them to shudder. But it had to be exposed, so that their healing could be directed to the right place.

They formed the points of a triangle around it, an arm's length apart from one another. At a word from Ariel they began.

They stared at the break in the wood, and power flowed out from each of them. Ariel burned even more brightly, and the other two began to glow as well. The lines of power between them thickened, grew visible. The three became one power, one magic that wrapped around the staff and held the severed ends together.

Every living thing on the island held its breath and waited, standing still as stone. Yet the stones themselves seemed to breathe, to contain a pulse of life. The island opened itself to the power of the three, and the magic filled the void that had been growing and gnawing at its heart for so many empty years.

Ariel was fire heat, smoke dance, the kiss of sun on snow, pain of birth and pang of death. He was love's heart and hate's arrow, the seething song of the sea, the cry of a gull, and the crushing roots of a tree. He was the will of every lightning strike, and he sent it out to the center of the pain.

Caliban was young again, laughing on the shore, imitating the shriek of an eagle as it plunged into the sea for its prey. Then he was running through the forest, playing tag with the spirits of the trees. He knew them all by name, and they loved him, no matter who his mother was, no matter what she had done. He was the island's child. He was the island's hope. The trees knew his voice, the air whispered his name, the mermaids sang him lullabies. This was his home, and he sent his love out into the pain.

Calypso was strong, stronger than they guessed, stronger than she knew. She had the strength of the stones and the force of the tides. The moon was her servant. Knowledge she did not know she possessed filled her mind and revealed the path she must take. She could take and shape and hold things to her will. She reached out and grabbed the staff, right around the wound.

They screamed, all of them, but the ties that bound them could not be broken. The staff knew her, and named her: Sycorax.

The island began to writhe.

V.iii.

"My life!" the staff cried into the pain that flooded all their minds. "Pay the price," it demanded. "Pay the price and make me whole."

"Take it from her, Caliban!" Ariel shrieked. "Only you have the power! Take it from her, now!" The spirit flailed desperately, unable to touch her.

Caliban tried. He grabbed the staff with both his hands and tried to wrestle it from Calypso. Sweat stood out on his brow, and still he could not pull it free. The earth was heaving beneath their feet. Ariel buffeted them with a wind, but it threw Caliban off balance instead of Calypso. He fell to the ground, losing his hold on the staff.

Both Caliban and Ariel were thrown from the magic, cut from the staff. The spell was done.

Caliban stared at her, horror washing over him. The ghost of Sycorax played across the features of this strange girl's face.

She looked triumphant, and mad. A wild, maniacal laugh broke from her lips and spilled into the wind whipping around them all. Then she crumpled to the ground, unconscious.

It took Caliban a moment to recover. The island grew steady once more, exhausted. Ariel stilled the wind, and Caliban crawled to Calypso's side. His face was grim. "Look at this," he said to the spirit.

The staff had been healed, but it had not gone to its new master easily. Calypso's right hand was now made of wood, up just past her wrist, and it was permanently fused to the staff. Her flesh had been taken for the healing. It was only because of her strength that she was still alive.

"We must kill her," Ariel said. "Kill her and free the staff." He raised his arm.

"You'll kill the island if you do," Caliban replied.

Ariel lowered his arm. "So," he said, dully, his colors fading to pale gray, "we are to be enslaved once again. It would be better to die, I think."

Caliban looked down at Calypso. Gently he pushed her dark hair away from her face. "How can she be related to me?" he asked. "Sycorax died long before she was born."

"Your mother had a daughter, older than you, born in a distant land. She sent me to see her once, to discover if everything was well with her."

He had a sister. A Greek sister. A witch, who had a child. This child. Calypso, the sailor nymph; his niece. "And was it?" Caliban asked.

Ariel shrugged. "She was a plain girl. Stayed in her rooms.

When I appeared she hid from me. Sycorax never sent me back."

Caliban looked down at Calypso. "She was a witch," he said. "People were cruel to her."

"Imagine that," Ariel said bitterly.

Caliban gently touched Calypso's face. His niece. His sister's child. An unknown sister, for certainly his mother had never mentioned her. Now he understood the bitter silence that came over Sycorax whenever she spoke about her life before the island, the life of her home. Her grief was not for linen and gold and other fine things. It was for her daughter.

And now the child of that daughter was here, caught in the suffering of her grandmother's magic. Caught by her same desire to possess and control. His mother had found a way to reach out from death and make a final grab at the power she had once held. The power that had held her. Calypso would be driven mad, just as his mother had been. She would twist and die.

He could not let that happen.

"Perhaps we can cut her hand off," Ariel said. His words tore Caliban's thoughts. "It would be best to do it now, while she sleeps."

Caliban considered the grim suggestion, but touching her again showed him that it was impossible. "Her life fuels the staff," he said. "It will not release her without demanding its price. If we cut her from it, both will die."

"And if we don't?" Ariel asked.

Caliban touched the sleeping face once more. "If we don't,

she will be taken by the staff, slowly. In time she will be nothing but wood."

Ariel grew brighter, flaring suddenly with malevolent glee. "She will be imprisoned in a tree," he said. "How appropriate."

Caliban gritted his teeth, biting into his patience to keep it from slipping away. "When her life is gone the staff will have nothing to sustain it. The healing will fail and the island will die."

"So, we are left with enviable choice. Will it be a quick death, or a slow one?" Ariel stared down at her callously. "We could bind her into sleep and let the island feed off her."

Bile rose in Caliban's throat. "What, turn the island into a parasite? Make us all a tapeworm huddled in a child's gut?" He threw his words at the spirit. He wished they were stones, wished they could hurt Ariel for making such a suggestion.

Ariel glared at him. "You want me to pity her? I have no pity left for wizards. She was the island's last hope, and she chose to kill us all. The blood of Sycorax," he spat. His flames burned white.

Caliban had to look away. He swallowed his revulsion and considered Ariel's idea. The staff would drain her whether she was asleep or not. It was probably merciful to bind her as Ariel suggested. But he could not bring himself to do it. The thought of her lying there while the staff slowly leeched the life force from her bones was unbearable. "There must be another way," he whispered.

"Don't be a fool," the spirit hissed. "She is not worth saving."

"She is a child," Caliban replied. "All children are worth saving."

Ariel sneered. "Such noble sentiments," he said. "It's the island I care about, not some witch-brat."

Calypso shifted restlessly. Ariel reached out an arm to cast the spellnet around her, but Caliban knocked it away. Her eyes flew open. The spirit flew upwards, his face boiling with terror and hatred. "Fool!" he shrieked, just before he vanished. "Treacherous, earth-born fool!"

Caliban took Calypso's good hand in his. "Everything's fine," he lied, his voice soothing. He stroked her hair. "How do you feel?" he asked. "Do you have any pain?"

Calypso watched his face, her eyes troubled and confused. Caliban repeated his words, hoping she'd understand. He remembered that she did not speak his language well.

"My son," the girl whispered, in a voice that seemed hardly her own. "Where is Caliban, my son?"

V.iv.

Caliban had lost his mother tongue long ago, but Calypso's words, spoken in Sycorax's own voice, stirred a forgotten understanding. Caliban gripped her hand, the left one, still flesh. Cold flesh, the warmth and strength pulled away. He rubbed it gently between his, quieting its trembling. "Hush, now," he whispered. "You need to rest. You need to be peaceful."

Clearly she was confused. Her lips moved soundlessly, as though they were trying to pluck words out of the air. He could not make out what she was trying to say.

"Can you tell me your name," he asked, gently.

"Sycorax," she said. Then her face twisted. "Calypso," she said. She looked angry. "I tell this to you before, my name it is Calypso."

"Of course," he said. "I forgot, that's all. I forget things."

"Yes," she responded, relieved, almost eager. "Me as well, forget things...." Her eyes drifted away, to the clouds. "I remember the sky over Greece," she added softly, in her own language.

She was so still that Caliban thought she would fall asleep, but soon her gaze turned back to him. Her expression grew hard, fierce. "Who are you?" she demanded. She pulled away from him and tried to rise.

It was then that she saw her hand. She touched it, puzzled. "Strange," she whispered. She looked at him uncertainly. "My hand, it is wood," she said. She laughed nervously, a wild note in her voice once more.

"It was the healing, Calypso," Caliban said, trying to keep her with him, trying to keep Sycorax away. "You took the staff in the healing and bound it to yourself."

She stared at him, her eyes wide, her left hand prying at the right's grip on the staff. "Yes, this happened," she said. She looked down at her hand, growing more desperate. "Take it, Caliban!"

"I will," he said. "But we must find a safe way. You are joined now—"

He broke off. She was staring at him, her pupils expanding in her eyes. Black eyes. His mother's eyes: mad and dangerous.

"Caliban," she said. "Caliban. Ban, Ban, Caliban."

"That's right, Calypso, it's me," he said, desperately trying to win the girl back.

"My son is Caliban," she said. She was speaking the language of his childhood once more, her eyes narrow slits of suspicion. "Who are you that has stolen my son's name from him? Give it back, wretch, give it back!"

"No, Calypso, no!" he cried, but he could not stop her. She

raised the staff and blasted him backwards, throwing him against a rock with such power that he felt a rib crack. Pain shot through him. Fire chased the air into his lungs and boiled it there before letting it sear its way back out. "Calypso," he croaked, "you must remember yourself. You are Calypso, whatever the staff tells you. You are Calypso."

She stared at him, her face twisting, wrenched by the two minds warring within her.

"Tell her, Calypso," he gasped. "Tell her that I am her son, full grown now, a man. Tell her she died and I grew up. Tell her, Calypso."

He didn't know if Calypso could do what he asked. He just knew that his mother would not harm him. She had died to protect him.

"Full grown," said the Sycorax face. She crawled toward him, grating the staff against the ground. Finally she reached him. "Full grown," she said again, reaching out to him with her left hand and touching his hair. "Hair like a ginger cat's," she said. "My Caliban." She stroked his face tenderly. "You're hurt," she said, suddenly puzzled.

"Yes," he replied. The word twisted strangely in his mouth. It felt as though each breath he took was tearing him apart.

"You can't be hurt," she said. She touched him with the staff's tip. Warmth rushed through him, soothing and sudden, warmth that caught the burning pain and swallowed it. In an instant the air that he drew in cooled his lungs. This was the mother he remembered. The mother who tried to be kind, no matter how fiercely her madness held her. He sat up.

Her face was gray. "You've drained yourself," he said, suddenly afraid. "You must rest, Calypso."

"Yes," she answered, slumping to the ground. He lifted her in his arms, folding the staff across her body. She was light, but he still staggered as he carried her. He took her into the hut and laid her upon Miranda's old bed, the one that he had slept in only last night.

She looked up at him. "That's better," she said. Her eyes closed. "Caliban," she said.

"Yes?"

"Stop calling me by that silly name."

He struggled to speak through the tightening in his throat. "Yes, mother," he whispered.

He sat down on the other bed and watched her. She was restless, twitching and muttering to herself in her sleep. Three times during the hour she startled full awake, each time soothed back to sleep by Caliban. Twice she was Sycorax, once Calypso. Every time she was frightened. "Caliban?" she would call. He would stroke her forehead and whisper that all was well, that all would be well.

He convinced her, at last. She fell into a deeper sleep, her breathing calm and regular.

He was not so easily comforted. He sat upon the bed, rubbing the palms of his hands against his temples. He was hungry again, but he was afraid to leave her. Ariel might be nearby, just waiting to bind her beyond his care.

He left the hut and went out to the fire. It was nothing but coals now. He fed it some more wood. The smoke made him dizzy. He needed food. Grimly he cast a sheltering spell over the hut. He must protect Calypso, whatever he felt about magic. There was a taste of metal in his mouth. That always came with spellcasting. It was sour and unnatural and he hated it.

He shook his head and left, swiftly, to forage for food. He was back within the hour, carrying fish, mushrooms, some plants, and his old cooking kettle, rescued from his cave. At a nearby spring he filled it with water. He had done this very thing thousands of times, making food for Prospero and Miranda. Well, now he would feed himself. And he would feed his niece. And then, somehow, he would cure her. He set about making a stew. It had just begun to bubble and give off a faint savory smell when Calypso awoke.

She screamed. It was shrill, panicked, the cry of someone waking into a nightmare. He was by her side in an instant. She was sitting upright, flailing with her right arm, trying to shake the staff from her hand.

"Shhh, Calypso, you're well, all will be well," he said, over and over, holding her. Finally her eyes cleared and she slumped forward, cradling the staff and her wooden hand against her heart.

"No, Caliban," she croaked. She lifted her eyes to his. "I be never well now, I think."

"Yes, you will," he insisted. "Come now and eat. You need to be strong."

She shuffled out with him, leaning heavily on his arm as they walked. The sunlight made her squint. He helped her sit on a rock. She held the staff away from herself, letting it hang and drag behind her. Caliban poured some stew into one of the wooden bowls left behind by Prospero. He sat beside her and placed an old spoon in her left hand. The awkwardness of eating brought fresh tears to her eyes. "Nevermind," he said, softly, "it's only for a little while."

Calypso must have been famished. She ate three bowls of the stew. When she finished the third, she slid down to the ground and rested her back against the rock. Caliban ate the rest, right out of the cooking kettle. He didn't want her to see how little was left for him. It didn't matter, anyway. He could make more later, when she slept again.

For the longest time they sat in silence, Calypso staring into the flames of the fire, Caliban watching her from beneath his lowered eyelids. He was grateful that Sycorax was gone. He hoped she would stay away.

Finally she looked up at him. "Tell me. This princess," she said, "she went into the water, yes?"

"Chiara," he said. He had forgotten about her. How could he have forgotten about Chiara? Grief and fatigue washed over him, compounded now by guilt. The emotions threatened to drown him. Only he was not drowned; Chiara was. "She was my daughter," he said.

"This I never know," Calypso said. "I think…people, they say she was princess, but no?" she added.

He shrugged. "She was," he said, "but she was an unusual child, and they often left her to my care. So she was mine, you see, no matter who her parents were." As he spoke he saw Chiara's seven-year-old face looking up at him, while she held out a baby bird. "Help me find its nest, Caliban," she'd said. "I don't want one of the cats to get it."

"Tell me about my sister," Caliban said. "Your mother, I mean. Tell me about her."

Calypso leaned her head back and closed her eyes. Caliban wondered if she was going to answer at all, when she said, "She always afraid. Always. She never left house. People, they see her…" She touched her forehead, searching for the word. "Her burn? This thing you make with the hot metal."

He shivered, understanding. "Her brand," he said, softly.

"Yes, this is it. Her brand. She think the people throw their rocks at her, like when she be a young girl."

Children had thrown rocks at him too, when he first had gone to Milan with Prospero. Before he realized how strange he looked. But he had never been afraid, only angry. The stars were his brothers. He had nothing to be ashamed of, back then.

Not like now.

"What did she love?" he asked, forcing his mind back to his unknown sister.

"My father," she replied instantly. Then she thought longer. "She love the snakes."

"Snakes?" he asked.

"Yes, also the ones that bite. She never let snakes be hurt, never. She talk to them. They sit on the rocks in the sun and she stand in the door, and she talk to them. She name them. The snakes, they be her one friends, I think."

He smiled. He had always liked snakes himself, their strong sinuous grace and speed, their darting tongues. He had kept one in the palace, until Prospero learned of it. The old man hated them. He had to set it free. Chiara had come with him. He remembered her holding the long, black snake gently in her hands as it wound itself around her arm and between her fingers. She stroked its back and then set it on the ground. It had lain there for a moment, tasting the air before it flashed away. "They never look back, do they, Caliban," she had said, wistfully. "No," he'd told her, "they live only in the moment. They don't remember." She had looked thoughtful then, and chewed on the tip of her braid. "Too bad for the snakes," she'd said.

"She love me, too," Calypso whispered.

"She never knew you," Caliban said, until he realized she meant her mother, and not Chiara. "Oh. My sister. Of course she loved you."

"She wish I had not the magic. She said it was gift-curse." She looked down at her hand. Caliban saw her flinch.

"Because of Sycorax, my mother. Her mother," he added. "I hate magic, too. I refused to use the staff when she died, because of what it did to her."

It was a dangerous comment to make. Calypso turned her face away, her body trembling. "I'm sorry, Calypso," he said, immediately. "I shouldn't have said that."

"Why?" she said, turning back to him. It was his mother's haggard face once more, speaking fluently in her own tongue. "You are right, Caliban. My magic destroyed me and everyone I loved. Except your father, of course." Then she began to laugh and sob at once, folding her left hand over her head and pressing her face against her chest, smothering her cries.

Caliban did not know what to do. If he called back Calypso, he would lose this chance to finally learn about his father. There was no Setebos. He had never been the son of a god. He'd faced that truth long ago. Perhaps now he could learn the truth.

But he could not let Calypso be swallowed up by Sycorax. He could not loose that madness on the island again. "Calypso," he said, reaching out to the girl, stilling her shaking shoulders with the heaviness of his hand. "Calypso," he said, "you are stronger than she is. She is dead and you are alive, Calypso. You rule yourself."

Her sobs grew quiet. Finally she lifted her head. Calypso was restored. For now.

V.v.

The deeps were quiet. Leviathan lay awake, but all of the heads were silent. Finally the central head spoke. "It is the third day," it said.

The horse head snorted softly, but said nothing.

"The third day," the goat head said. "The day life came to be. Resurrection day. The day of the triple goddess, of the three-part god."

"The day we finally get to eat," hissed the serpent head.

"And about time, too," the dog head laughed, barking in agreement.

The bearded head lifted and tilted to one side, as though listening. "I'd say not. There's life in her still."

"She may survive the trial," the horse head said.

"I hope so," grunted the armored head. "We haven't had a successful trial for over a thousand years, as the small ones count time. It gets dull."

"Successful!" the dog head sneered. "She's still a long way from success."

"Not as long as we may think," the central head whispered. "Listen. She grows wise."

They all looked within themselves. Even the serpent's mind began to feel the glow of excitement.

⌒

Chiara thought of nothing and knew everything. Her heart's pulse was that of the stars. She was caught up in the breath of the universe, part of its joyous exhalation.

I am nothing, she thought. *I am everywhere. I am not afraid anymore.*

"Really?" said the Leviathan. "Do you not fear the burn of our body digesting you? Do you not fear the weight of water crushing your bones once we have spat them out? Do you not fear having your eternal soul kept here, imprisoned in this dark and airless place?"

Chiara felt her way through the questions. "I do not," she said at last. She marveled at the truth of her answer.

Leviathan laughed. "Shall we believe, then," it said, "that you do not long to see the sun once more? That you do not yearn to walk freely again, to feel the arms of your beloved around you, to grow and live and taste the world? Do you truly not desire the richness of a full life?"

Chiara sifted the words of the Leviathan through her mind and heart. They fell away, husks of dreams that were no longer her own, pale and shallow against the great gasp of life she had just seen. What was the warmth of one small sun to her now? She was sister to the stars. She did not need life. She was life.

"I do not," she said. She was not even amazed at her own words. She feared nothing, she wanted nothing. She simply was.

Light blossomed in her mind, the light of the Leviathan, the light of the universe's core.

—*You are our child now*, the light said to her.

"Yes," she agreed. And then she added, "But I don't really know what that means."

—*Babies never do*, the light laughed.

"Babies?" she said.

—*You are to be reborn, Chiara. You have passed the guardians and found the treasure.*

"I have only found myself," she said.

—*Then you have found everything.*

She spun around, was pressed on all sides. Her mind shrank in on itself. She felt herself swept along in a current of light and confusion. There was pain, too, but most of it was not hers. It was the pain of birth.

And then she was surrounded by water once more. Before she could think, a scaly arm reached out and broought her gently before the faces of the Leviathan. She smiled at them, amazed that they were ever terrifying to her.

For a long time they regarded one another. She smiled at the differences among the heads, heard their unique voices in her mind. They were surprised, even pleased. She looked down and was amazed to see that she was still herself, human and small. "I thought I'd become a dragon," she said.

"You have," Leviathan answered, "in every way that matters." They smiled, showing all manner of terrifying jaws and teeth. Chiara grinned back at them affectionately.

"It has been a long time since one of our children walked on the face of the earth," Leviathan said.

She would have to go back. The small life that she had sloughed away twisted itself around her legs, pulling her back to reality. "What am I supposed to do there?" she asked. "I don't know how to be a dragon. I barely knew how to be a human being."

One of the heads bent down and nuzzled her. It had a tough golden hide and hundreds of teeth, but what she noticed most was the long, red beard that trailed from its jaws. That, and the kindness of its eyes. "You will learn," it said, encouragingly. "All our children find their place."

"But where will I go?" she asked, feeling suddenly overwhelmed.

A long goat-like head, heavy with curling horns, twisted toward her. "Wherever you choose," it said. "You are a dragon now. Wherever you go is the place you should be."

Memory stirred within her new mind. "But first I must heal the island," she said.

Images flashed through her mind, the brilliant speech of the Oldest. She saw the healing that had happened, with its terrible price. She spoke to the island, heard its bitter voice, its anger grown through years of suffering. "I will not release her!" it shrieked. "Calypso's blood will heal my wounds!"

"The island has gone mad," Chiara said, pulling her mind away.

"It has been so for many years now," Leviathan replied. "Now, it has found its voice."

Leviathan shifted slightly and Chiara saw the spell book, suddenly revealed between the beast's forepaws. She lifted it up. It belonged to her. She did not even need to open it to read it. The spells simply flowed into her, becoming her own knowledge. When she had swallowed them all, she put the book back down, to rest again in its place of protection.

"Go now," they said. "The upper world calls you. Take this," they added.

Chiara held out her hand and they dropped a pearl into it. It was perfectly round, rose-colored, and as big as a large apple. Her alchemical training told her what it must be. "The thunderball," she whispered.

"You have the right to wield it," they said. "Some day you will make your own. For now, take it as a mother's parting gift."

"Thank you," she whispered. And then she felt a great sadness, for she knew that she would never return to the deeps. Her realm would be somewhere else.

"Blessings, daughter," they replied.

She turned and began to walk home, cradling the pearl against her heart. She could have transported herself to the island with a thought. She felt the summons of the upper reaches, just as her new monster-mother had, but still she walked on, savoring the peace of the deeps. Every creature she met shied away from her.

Chiara came to the soul field. The mermaid was gone. Chiara

stood for a while, listening to the soft moans coming from the traps. With a word and a gesture she could free them all.

But she had lost her desire to help them. Their cries no longer tore at her heart. They were here because they chose to be here, because they wanted to be fooled. The siren's song had not really deceived them. Deep down they knew the peril of following the music beneath the waves. But they leapt anyway. The danger itself was a delight. And they each thought that they alone could survive the risk. The mermaid was right. They had given themselves away.

And then, with her new dragon knowledge, she discovered a strange truth. The souls had built their own cages. They were not woven out of metal, but of all the false hopes and empty wishes that had lived in their human hearts. The souls could free themselves. They were trapped because they were still caught by the lure of fool's gold.

But she could not tell them this. They wailed so loudly that they could no longer hear anything but the sound of their own sorrow. Chiara turned away from them. Perhaps, in time, they would find their own salvation.

It was surprising that the mermaid had left the field. Chiara threw out a spellnet, searching for the creature. At last she found her, up at the surface. She was singing up a storm with her two sisters.

And they were fighting Caliban.

Her young dragon wisdom evaporated. She was a girl once more, and the only person she had left in the world needed her.

V.vi.

The raging wind shook Caliban awake. It tore around him, screamed across the stones. Every joint of his body had seized, twisting and knotting him cruelly. He wrenched himself up. The grinding of his bones made him grit his teeth until his jaw ached and the tears welled in the corners of his eyes. He had no idea how long he had slept or even what day it was. The air stank of magic. He looked over at the other bed to check on Calypso.

She was gone.

In the pale dawn light, he looked around the room wildly, as though he might find her hiding in a corner or beneath a bed. He cursed himself for falling asleep. He did not know where to begin looking for her, and his body ached so badly that he doubted he could go far to find her.

Lightning ripped down the sky, piercing the water like a great trident. He began to run then, ignoring every cry from his tortured joints.

She was Sycorax, and she was attacking the ship.

"I curse you!" Sycorax screamed. "May my hatred be the last air that you breathe! May the waters smother you slowly, crushing you with their weight until you beg for death! May all your children and all your mothers waste away waiting for you to return, until they walk the earth as pale shadows, always searching for you, never finding you. May your homes be burned to the ground and a pain strike any lip that dares to utter your names. I curse you, now and forever!"

She pulled the fire from the sky and set the ship ablaze. A wailing cry went up, but it was quickly lost in the roar of the flames. She danced on the shore, flinging her bare feet high and laughing as the ship burned on the waves. They would regret leaving her here upon this godforsaken land.

"No!" cried a man's voice. She turned and saw a squat, lumbering creature moving awkwardly toward her across the rocks. He wore a cape of feathers. His arm was outstretched, words of power tumbled from his lips. He called down the rain. A deluge fell upon the ship, dousing the fire.

She leveled the staff at him, ready with the words needed to rend his bones from his flesh. Before she could speak she was thrown back upon the stones. A spirit of the air was before her, and in its hands a spellnet that would hold her fast. She turned her staff upon him, but he was torn away before she could utter a word.

The lumbering creature stood over her, protecting her. Tufts of gingery hair stood up around his ears. The sight made her pause. Confusion fell upon her once more. Years tumbled through her mind, a death, her death; a new mind surged forward, trying to control her.

The spirit of air shrieked. "She must be stopped, Caliban! You cannot hold her. She would have destroyed all the innocents on the ship!"

Caliban. Caliban must not be hurt. The thought singed her mind with its clarity. She bent herself around, closing the circle of pain.

~~~

"No, Calypso!" Caliban cried. He was frantic, trying to save his niece from his mother's fate and fend off Ariel. The shouts from the ship distracted him further. Ariel was right about that; the ship must be protected. He pulled the green handkerchief from beneath his robe and loosed its knot once more.

The last faint whisper of Prospero's breath went out across the waters, still powerful enough to catch Ariel in its tide and sweep both spirit and ship out to sea. He knew that Ariel would be back soon. In the meantime, he had to help Calypso. He knelt beside her and tried to unclench her left hand from her ankles, to break the punishment she was inflicting on herself. He was gentle at first, but in the end he had to tear her hand away with all his strength. She gasped when he did it, whether out of relief or because of the wrenching twist of her flesh he could not tell.

She collapsed immediately into unconsciousness. He lifted her up and over his shoulder and stumbled with her to his cave.

Ariel had no power here, in the deep places of the earth. He could not enter without growing thin and pale. He'd done it once, long ago, on Sycorax's command. When she saw that Ariel could not serve her, she'd sent him away. The spirit had never come back to the cave since.

Caliban spread his feather cloak over the old branch bed and then laid Calypso down upon it. In no time he had lit the small fire, bringing some warmth and light into the cave. He went back to Calypso and examined her hand. It would be bruised, but he had not broken any of the small bones. He supposed that she had her hardy existence as a sailor to thank for that. There was sweat on her brow, and she was muttering in Greek. He could not make out anything that she was saying.

Quickly he went to the far corner of the cave, to a dark crevice where the light of the cooking fire never penetrated. There he felt about until he found the small earthenware vessel he'd been looking for. He lifted it carefully and brought it out to the fire. He brushed the thick layer of dust off it and removed the lid.

There was some left. Not a lot, but enough. It was a powder Ariel had brought him when he was a boy, a medicine for his mother. Poppy powder. It was the only time he had colluded with the spirit against his mother. Ariel had told him that it would take away pain and bring sleep. Caliban would sprinkle it on his mother's food when she had gone too long without rest.

Carefully he measured a small amount of the powder and mixed it with some water in his old wooden drinking cup. He lifted Calypso's head and gently encouraged her to swallow the liquid. Its bitter taste made her wince and cough, but still he was satisfied that she'd taken enough to help her. He sat beside her, his hand on the pulse in her left wrist, and watched her. Her breathing slowed, her muttering ceased. She slept, a smile curving her lips. Caliban knew that the powder brought dreams with it. His mother would recount them in the morning. He wondered what Calypso would dream about. He hoped they would be Calypso's own dreams, and not the visions of abandoned palaces that had filled his mother's nights.

He rose, his tired limbs aching. He wanted to lie down and sleep again, even take some of the mixture himself. But that escape was not for him, not now.

He went out from the cave, to face Ariel.

The air was electric with suspended spells. Ariel was not alone. He had been joined by the mermaids. The three sisters lay in the shallows of the shore, their wet hair streaming over their naked chests, their tails concealed by the waves.

Caliban bowed to them. They each bared their teeth in response, ghastly imitations of a smile.

"You have something we need, Caliban," Peisinoe said. Her green eyes glared at him coldly. "Give her to us, Caliban," she said.

For a moment he almost turned and obeyed her. Few could resist her suggestions, even fewer her commands. It was she who called sailors from their ships to their deaths, persuading them that she was a fair human maid, and not the green-skinned, green-haired water-witch their eyes first spied. But some far corner of his mind remembered the trick of her speech, and so he was able to stand against her will.

"I cannot," he replied.

The three sisters threw back their heads and howled, their voices piercing him. He covered his ears with his hands, trying to shut out the madness they invoked. Ariel gestured them to stop. Amazingly, they did. Caliban let his hands fall.

"You'll madden her further," Ariel was saying to them.

"She's asleep," Caliban said.

Ariel turned to him. "You have spelled her, then?" He looked disbelieving.

Caliban shook his head. "Drugged her," he answered, "with the sleeping powder you gave me long ago for my mother."

"So," said Ariel. His eyes narrowed in thought. "That will not hold her for long. When she wakes, what then?"

"Then I will feed her. Calypso will be hungry."

"And Sycorax?" Ariel's eyes burned. "What if it is Sycorax who awakes? Will you feed her more poppy and hope that she returns to the land of the dead?"

"My mother is dead. It is only her memory that returns." Caliban's words sounded hollow to his own ears.

"Her memory, earth-born?" It was Aglaope who spoke, her beautiful face pinched and mocking. She was the fairest of the three, her skin pale and gleaming, her hair a thick curling purple river flowing down her back. "A powerful memory, burning the ship and calling down the storm."

"As you are also threatening to do," Caliban replied. "I can smell it in the air. But you should know that all the rain and all the wind in heaven will not convince me to give up my niece. She is innocent."

"Innocent, Caliban?" It was Thelxepeia who spoke now, her words, as ever, as smooth and soothing as milk. "Ariel tells us that she stole the staff in the mending. She claimed the power. Now, it seems, she must pay the price. The island wills it."

"She's a child," Caliban replied stubbornly. "She did not know what she was doing. She was only trying to protect herself, to make a place for herself. She is not my mother."

"But her blood is the same, and the island claims it. You don't know her, Caliban, however much you may pretend and call her "niece." She is not the child you lost beneath the waves. She is Sycorax's blood, and she stole with Sycorax's will. Her life is forfeit. Spill her blood, and let the island go free."

"The island needs a queen," Caliban began.

"We've had enough of queens, and kings, and the rule of mortal wizards. They bleed the land, bleed us all," Aglaope said. "It is her turn to bleed."

"Never," replied Caliban.

The storm fell again, a smothering blanket of wind and water. Waves rose up, empty maws ready to devour him, drag him down to the sirens' lair. He pulled his own protection around him, fighting his way back to the cave. Hail pelted him, one large ball of ice striking against his temple and stunning him. He fell to his knees.

"Submit!" he heard Ariel cry. "Submit, moon-calf!"

The ancient taunt spurred him on. His rose back to his feet and staggered toward the cave.

"Call down fire!" Aglaope cried. He could hear her shrill voice even above the fury of the storm. "Summon the Leviathan, and we three elements will form the hurricane. That will shake him loose!"

He fell once more, hearing the words of power Ariel was screaming into the riot of wind and water. The earth shifted beneath his feet. Dragon power had been called, and it was awakening. He felt as though his heart would burst with rage and despair. "Bring on your dragon!" he cried, his words whipped away even as he spoke. "Let me see Chiara's killer!"

The sea seemed to split. Caliban stumbled, Ariel fell to the ground, and the three mermaids flung themselves upon one another as their minds were flooded with dragon speech. Caliban saw eyes everywhere in his mind; huge, fiery, reptilian eyes that burned through him, exposing the smallness of his soul. He covered his head with his arms and cowered on the beach. The air was cleaved with a single lightning bolt. It tore a hole through the storm, leaving everything around the warring powers strange and still. Thunder rumbled around the edges of the spell-bubble.

He lifted his head and stared. Walking across the water, holding the thunderball in her hand, was Chiara.

V.vii

Caliban stood and ran to meet Chiara, not realizing his folly until he was knee deep in water. He began to laugh. He laughed at his wet knees, laughed at life, at Chiara's life that was not lost but was kept, held, transformed, returned. "You have come back!" he cried, and laughed again, because of course she knew that.

She ran to him, shouting joyfully. Her feet splashed across the surface of the sea, leaving small footprints of bubbles that melted away almost as quickly as they formed. It was such an astonishing sight that he stepped backward and fell down into the water. In a moment she was beside him. She pulled him to his feet and threw her arms around his neck. Her strength was incredible. He felt as though she could snap him in two as easily as he might snap a twig. She kissed his cheek and her lips burned where they touched his flesh. With a great effort, he grasped her arms and held her away from him, searching her face.

She was herself, and not herself. Her features were

unchanged. She still smiled her lopsided smile. Her hair still hung in heavy, lank braids on either side of her head. But her eyes…he puzzled about it for a moment. They were still hazel. Their shape had not changed. Their lashes still clustered thickly about them, looking for all the world like a spider's legs. But the mind that looked out from behind them was altered. It was no longer simply intelligent. It was ancient, and wise. It was born of the fires found at the earth's core.

"You are a dragon," he said.

She looked down at the great pearl she held in her hand, its rosy surface wet and luminescent. "I am," she said softly. She looked back at him, a sudden sadness twisting her face. "It was the only way out, Caliban. It was the only way."

"Are you apologizing?" He lifted her chin with his forefinger. "You have become greater than I ever dreamed for you. Why do you think I'd be anything but happy?"

She searched his eyes. Suddenly his mind was filled with her dragonspeech. "Because you have been my father, and I am no longer your child. Because in my birth, I also died. I will never be the person either of us thought I'd be."

"You are alive," he replied, his own mind-speech sounding frail, pathetic. "You are still Chiara, new and rare. I will love the dragon as well as I loved the girl."

Her mind withdrew from his. She gazed at him, her eyes dark and unreadable. "I am changed," she said. She turned away and looked at the mermaids cringing upon the shore and Ariel once again hovering above the waves. "You summoned me," she said, her voice as cold as any snake's. "What do you want?"

They were silent at first. Then Ariel replied. "We summoned the Leviathan. We have the right."

"I have come in my mother's place," she replied. "What do you want from me?"

The spirit flickered unsteadily. "We claim the Sycorax-girl Caliban has hidden in his cave. Her blood is forfeit to the island. Her rule must be stopped."

Chiara tilted her head to one side, as though listening to distant music. She raised her left hand and laid it on Caliban's brow. As she did so, she turned to him. All traces of laughter were gone from her face. "I must see everything that has happened, Caliban. Will you let me?" He nodded, uncertain. With a jolt, he felt his memories of the past days tumble over themselves. They were being pulled from his mind, viewed, and then tossed back to him. It seemed that he could feel them pile up in his brain, a small discarded refuse heap. He tried to jerk his head away, but she held him fast. In another instant she was done. She lowered her hand, reaching down and squeezing his fingers before letting go and turning back to the others. He stepped away from her.

"The island is taking her life anyway," Chiara said. "Why do you wish to hurry it? Caliban can contain her."

"She will destroy us all," one of the mermaids hissed. It was the purple one, the one she had wrestled with on the seafloor a lifetime ago.

"Aglaope," Chiara said aloud, tasting the ancient name on her tongue while she tasted her new understanding of the creature in her mind. "I have said Caliban will contain her. Your war with him is finished. Be gone."

The mermaids opened their mouths to protest. Chiara frowned. "Be gone!" she said again, this time with the full force of her dragonspeech. They turned at once, all three, and disappeared beneath the waves. The storm, held at bay, began to shred apart at the edges. The sun returned.

"This is not finished," Ariel said. His colors grew more vibrant with his anger. "Caliban cannot control her, not with all the poppy powder in the world. The next time she breaks free, I will be here."

He vanished, with a clap of distant thunder. Chiara shrugged, and turned toward Caliban. He was watching her warily.

She smiled, this time wanly. "Take me in to see her, Caliban," she said.

He hesitated, but only briefly. *It's still Chiara*, he told himself. And then he noticed that he thought of her as "it." He swallowed and said, "This way." He was afraid.

She followed him, crouching low to enter the darkness, even though there was plenty of room. She stood for a moment in the weak, ruddy light of the small fire. "Higher," she said, stretching out her hand to the flames. They instantly responded, burning high and bright, flooding the shadows with yellow light.

Caliban grimaced. "A pretty trick," he said. He had always hated the use of magic in practical matters. It was lazy and careless. Magic was a sacred art, not a common tool. That was his mother's mistake. He had never thought it would be Chiara's.

She knew his thoughts. "It is no trick, Caliban. The fire belongs to me. All fire, everywhere, is part of me now. I am no longer human. Let me see your niece."

He stared at her. She looked back at him. Shadows played across her face. Her familiar features had begun to blur and change. Wordlessly he turned away and knelt beside the sleeping girl, taking Calypso's good hand in his and stroking it gently. Chiara crouched down on the other side of her. She stared at Calypso's face, slack in its drugged sleep, and at the wooden hand that clutched the staff forevermore.

For the first time, Caliban saw them together. His heart was split.

V.viii.

Chiara touched the staff, then the hand that gripped it. The lore of the spellbook flashed through her mind, as well as the dragon knowledge that was growing within her. She felt the universe spin and saw the fountains of stars that flowed out into space. She was part of all that burning fire, and she wanted to be with it, in it. She did not want to be tied here to earth by this foolish girl and her wooden hand. Her gaze slipped to Caliban. Her love for him still held her, a small fire in its own right. "There is a way to break the bond," she said.

"I will not let her die," Caliban said, fiercely.

"Her life does not need to be lost," Chiara replied.

She felt his suspicion. "And her mind?" he asked.

He knows I am gone from him, she thought, sadly. *He cannot love a dragon.* She looked down, shielding her eyes, making herself speak gently. Making herself sound human. "I do not know about her mind. Sycorax has scarred her, I think. I cannot tell you how much can be healed. You may have a difficult time caring for her."

"Me?" He stared at her. "Won't you help me?"

She rose abruptly, tired of talking, tired of pretending to be who she once was. "Keep her sleeping," she ordered. "There are things I must do to prepare. Bring her to the place of the staff's making, where the guardian tree once stood. Wait there for me today, when the sun is at its highest. Do not be late, Caliban."

She left, and did not look back. Once outside Chiara, wrapped in her magic, flew, a fiery arrow, to the end of the world.

To Glass Mountain.

It wasn't glass, but amber. It was the land of the dead, the sanctuary of dragons, the home of the phoenix. Ravens circled it, crying out her arrival in their strange prophetic voices. The mountain was wondrous to Chiara's human eyes, familiar to her dragon's mind. She landed on its summit, the ravens settling around her in a haphazard circle. A chance memory made her smile. "A conspiracy of ravens," she said aloud. As a girl she'd always loved the names given to groups of creatures. As a girl...that was a lifetime ago. She waited, unmoving, while the ravens whispered and peered at her.

There was a burst of fire, of sunlight, so bright that she knew her human eyes would never see again. They were seared to ash in their sockets. She felt some pain. Or rather she felt a great deal of pain, but it seemed to come from far away and belong to someone else. No darkness fell with her new blindness. Instead, her mind was flooded with light, so white and piercing that every thought she ever had, and all the new dragon wisdom she had been given, was seen once more in a grand cacophony of knowledge.

She felt a breath, warm and spiced, blow across her face. Something hard, like small stones, was placed in each empty eye socket. A word was whispered in a speech that could be uttered only by the phoenix. The stones grew hot and expanded, filling the sockets. This pain was real and near. There was no distance between her suffering and herself. Yet Chiara stood still, her hands clenched. Images began to swim their way into her waiting brain. In another moment they grew clear. The pain faded.

She could see once more.

Her new eyes had been made from the amber of the mountain. They were golden, their pupils slitted like a snake's. She saw the old world in a new way. Her eyes refracted the light, split every image. Everything was a sum of its parts, and now she could look at the miniscule details. Each raven had a rainbow aura, each cell of its body revolved around a microscopic sun.

She could see the universe within every living thing.

Chiara blinked and looked at the phoenix. It was large, its wingspan stretching wide. Its feathers were red and gold, flecked with the blue-white of the hottest flame. Only the tips of its long, plumed tail were blackened. It folded its wings and sat down, smoothing its chest with its golden beak.

"You came swiftly," it said. "All the other transformed ones waited at least a year before coming."

"I can see why," Chiara replied, dryly.

The phoenix laughed, its tones high and fluting. "I'd wondered if a dragon would ever be born from humankind. I watched your trial with a great deal of interest. You were hardly the most likely candidate. But then the likely ones almost never succeed," it added philosophically.

Chiara stretched in the warmth. The pain in her eyes was now completely gone. She felt deeply content.

"Where will you go now?" the phoenix asked her. "There is a wide world, youngling. For you, there are many wide worlds. What will you do first?"

She felt her happy mood slide away. "I have to go back to the island. There's something I promised to do."

The phoenix ruffled its feathers. "Why tie yourself to mortals?"

"Love," she said.

"You have a poetic nature, then?" It turned its head to examine her more closely with one of its azure eyes.

Chiara grinned. Her teeth against her lips were newly sharp. She wondered how else she was changing. "Perhaps," she replied. She was suddenly impatient. "I must go," she said. "I said I'd return for midday."

The phoenix blinked. "You are impetuous, aren't you? Well, go. It is your right, of course."

Chiara shrugged her shoulders and stooped down. The surface of the mountain was smooth, but she quickly found the small crack she sought. She dug her nails into the amber, seeing in her mind the object she wanted, speaking the name of it into existence.

"Knife," she said. And there it was in her hand, a smooth dagger made entirely of amber, without flaw.

"The blade of the sun," the phoenix said, clearly troubled. "It has never been wielded before."

"There should be no need for it ever again," Chiara replied.

"I hope you are right," said the phoenix. "Such things, being forged, demand their own life. You trouble me, Chiara-Who-Was."

Chiara stared down at the knife. She felt no faltering in her will. "Don't worry," she said. "I know what I'm doing."

"So be it," the phoenix replied. "Go well, bright star."

Chiara lifted herself away. The ravens flew with her. They looked like an escort of doom, but they were good company and made her cheerful.

V.ix.

He cradled Calypso in his arms, but it was her drugged sleep that held her tightly. He would not let her go. He would not lose another child. Because the dragon-girl was right; Chiara was gone. That new creature could rifle through his mind as easily as if it were a stack of papers. Not just could. Would. Did. She had read his mind as it suited her purpose, because reading it was faster than waiting for him to tell her about the last three days. He was just a tool to be used and set aside.

He looked down at Calypso's sleeping face. She needed him. And when the staff was removed she would need him even more. He stroked her cheek. They could live together here, on the island. He'd build them a new home, a better one than the hut he'd made for Prospero. She could help him, perhaps. Or she could watch and grow strong again.

They could have the life he'd imagined for himself and Chiara. Calypso wasn't fleeing from a royal life. She was lost, and now they had found one another. They could be at peace here. There would be no guilt to haunt them.

He shook his head. He was spinning the same old fairy tale: two happy innocents, an island idyll. He examined the hand around the staff. It looked like the wood had begun to creep further up her arm. She lived under his mother's curse, brought down on her by her own greed. There was no paradise, even here on his magical island home. He was an old fool to imagine otherwise.

He went outside. It would be several hours before the sun reached its highest point. He did not want to move Calypso until he absolutely had to. She was ill. Ill people had to rest.

It was a beautiful day. The sun was warm, the sea was still, what little wind there was blew gently. There was no trace of the chaos that had just wracked this shore.

He sat down upon his old rock. The sun on his back warmed him to his core. He closed his eyes. Perhaps Chiara really would save Calypso. Then they could all stay here, together. He frowned. Something tugged at his memory, but he could not catch it. Nevermind. Maybe everything would be well. Maybe he could come to love the dragon, as he said he would. Maybe....

He opened his eyes again. The sea was still calm. But he was not fooled. "I know you're here," he said.

There was no reply at first. He'd surprised her, no doubt. Then the surface of the sea rippled. A familiar green head broke through, close to the shore. Even from this distance he could tell she was glaring at him.

"Hello again," he said. "Have you come back to finish your war with me?"

She bobbed in the water, looking for all the world like a seal. "I am not here to fight, Caliban."

"I'm glad to hear it, Pisces," he said. He hadn't been able to say Peisinoe when he was small. It had always made her laugh. Later, when Prospero told him it was the name for the sign of the fish, he'd laughed as well. But there was no smile on either of their faces today, no matter how pleasantly they spoke to each other.

She stared at him, silent once more. He shrugged his shoulders in irritation. All these unearthly beings were getting on his nerves. Between dragons, spirits, and mermaids he was beginning to miss Naples.

"What is it you want, then? I'm not much in the mood for conversation," he said at last.

"Listen to you. There's nothing wild about you anymore."

"No, there isn't. You're right. But here I am, all the same. This is my home. The dragon…I mean Chiara…says she will free the staff. When she does, I will claim it. I will not leave you again."

He only realized that he'd made the decision when he spoke the words. Of course he would be king. It was his fate. It was his birthright. His face twisted at the irony. After all this time he found that he was just like Ferdinand. He was born to be king. It was what his mother had always said. It was the specter he'd been running from his whole life. Well, now he would take it up, just as he had taken up Prospero's cloak.

"Oh, aren't we fortunate?" The mermaid's voice, usually so smooth and gentle, was rough with sarcasm. "The queen is dead, or soon will be at any rate. Long live the king."

He shook his head. "Calypso will not die," he replied.

"Somebody will," she said.

Fatigue swept over him. "No, Pisces. I said I will be king. The island does not need to take a life."

Peisinoe looked at him pityingly. "It's too late for that, Caliban. The island must be restored. The price must be paid."

"The price," he repeated. Anger began to crisp along his frayed nerves. "My mother is dead. Prospero is dead. The island has no right to demand any more lives. It will be healed. Now go away, Pisces," he finished. It took all his effort not to fling a stone at her head.

"You poor human man," Peisinoe said. Then she slipped away beneath the waves.

He looked out at the empty sea, letting the stillness calm him. He sat for some time. Nothing disturbed him, not even a seabird. That was strange. It was a fair day. Where had all the small living things gone?

The rocks crunched behind him. He turned, and then leapt up. Calypso was coming toward him. She staggered, still under some of the effects of the poppy. In her good hand she carried the cormorant cape. She used the staff to steady herself. Somehow that struck Caliban as ridiculous.

But at least she was Calypso. "You should not be up," he said, arriving at her side in three bounds. He tried to steer her back to the cave, but she shook him off.

"I want to be up," she said. At least that's what he thought she said. She was speaking in Greek again. Realizing this, she tried to switch back to Italian. "I have your…" She waved the cape, unsure of the word. "For you," she finished. Then she tried to put it around his shoulders.

"Thank you," he said, helping her. The cape felt silly again. Calypso swayed slightly. "Sit here," he said, trying to guide her to the rock.

"No," she answered, shaking his arm away again. "I don't want to sit. I want to go to the place."

"The place," he repeatedly blankly.

Her face rippled in frustration, almost becoming Sycorax, but sliding back into Calypso. "The dragon girl, she told you to bring me to the highest place…" Her voice trailed off, unsure. "To the place of the making," she corrected herself.

So, she had heard them. That was unsettling. He did not think anything could penetrate the poppy haze. Perhaps Ariel was right. He could not control her.

"This way, then," he said. "It's a long walk. The ground can be rough. But we'll go slowly."

She nodded, her face pinched with determination. "Let's go," she said.

It was difficult, nearly impossible. It wasn't just that he and Calypso had to tramp over brush and stones; they also had to fight their way through trees that still remembered their ancient hurt. Both of them were cruelly lashed by the leafless branches. They were driven to a marshy area, which they were forced to skirt around. It felt as though the island was doing everything it could to stop them. And frequently they did stop. Calypso often grew faint and had to rest.

At one point Sycorax came out and began yelling curses at

one particular tree. It was immediately blighted. From a great ancient thing it crumpled into a twisted, wilted, blackened lump. It looked like a heap of dead snakes. Caliban grabbed the girl by the arms and shook her. He was terrified, and so desperate to call back Calypso that he made her teeth rattle. She fell down, stunned by the force of his shaking, then she vomited up what meager food she had left in her stomach.

He was horrified with himself. But the face that lifted its gaze to meet his was Calypso's. In the midst of his guilt, he was tremendously relieved.

And he knew, as much as it disgusted him, that he'd shake her again if Sycorax came back.

They had to rest longer, until Calypso said the dizziness had passed. Caliban looked at her anxiously. He could tell that his concern annoyed her. He cast about for something to say.

She stared at the dead tree in front of her. "I do not like her," she said. She turned to Caliban. "My grandmother. I do not like her. I see, with her, why the people of my home call "witch." I see why they throw stones."

It was hard to argue with her. "She wasn't always like that, Calypso," he said. "She loved me. She was always kind to me."

Calypso shrugged. "It is easy, I think, to love the child. But my mother…" She looked away. "Sycorax, my grandmother, did not love her, I think. So my mother…" She let her sentence fall away, unfinished. It didn't matter. Caliban knew what she meant to say. It was hard to imagine what would have made Sycorax abandon his sister.

He flinched. Parents did abandon their children. They even sent them into the ocean to become dragons.

"We walk again," Calypso said, dragging herself back to her feet.

He led the way once more. Soon they had to fight their way through thorn bushes. By the time they cleared their way past them, they were both bleeding on their arms and faces. One of Calypso's eyes was swelling from a particularly nasty scratch on her eyelid. She was lucky it hadn't blinded her.

At last, impossibly, they came to the summit, to the place where the tree once stood. The blasted stump was there, the ground around it stripped bare. The earth had been burned away, and the skeleton stone exposed. He was not welcome here. No one was, no mortal or magical being. It was a place of pain.

And it remembered Sycorax. The ground heaved beneath their feet, as though the island wanted to toss them off into the sea. They clutched each other while they lay on the bare stone. Caliban stared up into the sky. The sun was nearly overhead. It should not be much longer before Chiara returned.

Calypso's face was white with strain. She began to mutter incoherently. He held her in his arms, wishing that he'd brought more of the poppy powder with him. It had been foolish to leave it. Maybe he could not control her, but at least he could have eased her suffering.

There was nothing he could do about it now. The island shook again, like an irritated dog. Lightning licked around the sky, strangely white against the clear blue. He kept expecting Ariel to appear, but the spirit stayed away. Chiara must have frightened him more than he'd revealed. Well, so much the better.

Again the island rattled its bones. He heard trees falling in the distance. Calypso moaned and covered her head with her good hand. Caliban tried to make soothing noises. They were useless.

More lightning crackled. It passed so closely over their heads that their hair stood on end. Calypso's muttering grew worse.

"He will not win…it is mine to take…this power…he will suffer…I will make him…be strong…I will have it again…" She grew more restless, her speech less comprehensible. She went back to moaning, and then she began to cry.

Caliban wanted to cry, too, but all his tears were gone.

V.x.

He looked to the sky. The sun was directly above them. The island would shake itself to pieces if they stayed much longer. If Chiara did not return soon, he would leave. This place made Calypso suffer too badly.

As if in summons to his thought, he saw a dark spot appear in the sky.

"She can fly," he said aloud. He laughed. Chiara had always wanted to fly. He felt giddy with the strangeness of it all. He waved his arm, showing her that he was here, that they were both here. The dark spot came closer and seemed to split apart. At its center was Chiara. There were birds flying with her. As they got nearer, he saw that they were ravens. He had to shield his eyes from the glare.

In another moment she landed. The ravens wheeled around her, brushing her with their wingtips, croaking in their ancient speech. Caliban ran to her, thinking that she was under attack.

But the birds lifted away, a flapping, boiling black cloud.

Then he saw her face, and a hum filled his ears and wiped all his thoughts away. The skin was raw, the flesh around her eyes and on her cheeks oozing painfully. Her eyes themselves… he could not even think, at first, about her eyes. They were slitted, serpentine. They were not Chiara's eyes at all.

"It's all right, Caliban," she said, speaking to his obvious thoughts. "It does not hurt anymore, no matter how it may look to you. I am content. Here," she said, bending down, turning her face from his, "help me stand her up. We need to prop the staff on the stump of the tree."

The ground beneath them twisted and heaved. "I don't think it will let us," he said. He could not look at her face as he spoke.

"It will obey me," she replied, her voice grim.

And it seemed she was right. The island grew still. Together, they lifted Calypso and placed the end of the staff squarely in the center of the stump. Calypso shuddered and hung limply from her foreign, wooden hand.

"Cut it off," she whispered. "I don't want it anymore."

"Hold her still," Chiara said. She placed her own left hand over Calypso's wooden one. Then, from a pocket, she pulled out a knife. It gleamed in the sun, warm, dangerous.

And suddenly he saw what she meant to do.

"No," he said. "There has to be another way."

"There isn't. Don't fuss, Caliban. My life is my own to give. Help me, or don't help me. Either way, Calypso will be saved."

He felt himself sway, watched the color drain from the

world. "No," he repeated. "I won't lose you again. You've already given your life once, Chiara. That should be enough."

"I agree," she said, with a hollow laugh. "But it appears that it is not."

So, Pisces was right. Somebody would die today.

He stared at her helplessly. "How will you do it?" he asked, at last.

"I'll reverse the spell Sycorax made with her moon-magic. This is magic of the sun, the source of all life. With it my life will feed the life of the tree. Calypso will be restored."

In a daze he nodded. Calypso leaned heavily against him. He shifted her weight so that he could move as needed.

Calypso woke then, screaming in wordless agony. Chiara tightened her grip on the wooded hand, then drew back her right, the amber knife gleaming in its grasp. With a word she drove it in – through Caliban's hand, through her own, through the hand of wood, through the heart of the staff. They all cried out in unison.

"Caliban," Chiara whispered, her mindspeech weak. "What have you done?"

"I've made my own choice," he answered. "My life for yours, for hers. The staff will choose me. I am the closest of Sycorax's blood. I belong here."

He smiled into Chiara's golden eyes. They were as beautiful as the green had been, really. And she had needed him after all. "I have a dragon for a daughter," he said.

The staff took root in the stump. The shock of it made them all cry out. Caliban, Chiara, Calypso, Sycorax; all became joined with the tree. Together they suffered, and loved, and hoped. Branches began to sprout from the wood of the staff. Its roots drew water. Buds appeared and burst forth into leaf and blossom. The island rejoiced.

And Caliban died.

He died laughing. "It is my birthright!" he shouted. The cormorant cape gleamed in the sun. His eyes blazed with joy. "I have come home," he said.

The three women held him in their hearts until his last breath. His life passed out to the tree. Then Sycorax was gone, her memory also slipping back into the tree, healing the wound she had made so long ago.

⟊

The knife fell out of the tree, and from the joined hands of Calypso and Chiara. But it stayed in Caliban's flesh. It was part of him, forever piercing, forever held in his grasp. Chiara knelt and touched the blade, the wound. Both were still warm. "His strength was always in his hands," she whispered. "And in his heart."

She discovered that her new eyes could not weep. She placed her newly scarred hand against his face, tracing the pattern of birthmarks down his throat. She'd never touched them before, she realized, though she'd always wanted to. "You were beautiful, Caliban," she whispered. Her eyes grew hotter, but still no soothing tears fell.

Calypso knelt beside her. Her hand was normal again, but

scarred as well. "He was my uncle," she said, wonderingly. "I say, he—" she repeated in Italian.

"I understand," Chiara said, interrupting her.

"You speak Greek," Calypso said. She stared at Chiara, then dropped her gaze when their eyes met.

"Apparently," Chiara replied. "I'm a dragon. I think I speak everything, now."

Calypso forced herself to look into Chiara's eyes. "You saved me," she said.

"Caliban saved you," Chiara replied.

If Calypso had healed the staff properly, Caliban would still be alive. He would be the island king. They could have lived here together. They could have been content.

But Chiara's dragon wisdom brushed these foolish thoughts away. If the staff had only been mended, Sycorax's ghost would still have been uneasy. The island would have remained enslaved. The staff would have corrupted Caliban. Calypso would have been alone, child of a madman.

A circle had no end.

Chiara reached out and touched the tree. It was strong. Its roots were deep. She looked up. Its branches stretched out, giving shelter, giving praise. Caliban's soul was here. He was not dead. He was only changed. And she knew, as well, that he was truly happy, at last.

She smiled at Calypso. "Help me move his body."

"Shouldn't we leave him here?" Calypso asked. "Isn't this where he belongs?"

"No," said a voice behind them. They turned. Ariel was there, in rainbow glory. "This is where he lives, now. But the earth of him must go back to the earth of the island."

"His cave," explained Chiara. Calypso nodded in understanding.

Ariel raised his hand. "No," Chiara said. "This is a mortal task."

The spirit frowned, then nodded. "Goodbye, brother," he said. Then he disappeared.

Together, Chiara and Calypso lifted Caliban's body, heavy and awkward, and between them carried him down to his cave. It was an arduous job. The island no longer fought against them, but the way was still rugged and treacherous. Even when they fell, and they fell often, Chiara refused to use any magic to help. It was her way to honor him, to do this last human thing as he would have wanted it done. They spoke to one another only to plan their way through difficult spots. At last they reached the cave.

They carried him inside and laid him down on his bed of branches. Calypso pulled at a long straw that had become tangled in her hair during their struggle to get to the cave. Deftly she tied a knot in it, twisting it with her clever sailor's hands. "It's a bowline," she said. "The king of knots. It always holds, but when it's time to leave, it slips free."

Chiara took the straw and placed the loop of it around the knife embedded in Caliban's hand. "Come away, now," she said to Calypso. They left the cave. It took only a word and a gesture to seal the entrance.

V.xi.

Calypso stood on the shore, her back to the cave's entrance. The ship was gone, of course. And now she had no power. It had been burned out of her in the sun-magic of the tree-making. She felt hollow and weak. She was alone on this island with no hope of escape and no way to survive, other than by her own wits. Her wits were sharp enough, but it was a lonely prospect nonetheless.

But she was not alone. She was alone with a dragon.

She shivered and wrapped her arms around herself. The tingling in her right hand was almost gone. She supposed that it was finally remembering how to be flesh. She looked down at the scar that slivered the center of both the back and the palm. It was a thin, neat line. It looked ancient, like the vague memory of a childhood injury. She touched it with her left hand, half expecting it to be still hot. It was not, of course.

Calypso smiled nervously. "My magic is gone," she said. "How will I protect myself?"

"I have enough magic for everyone," Chiara said, flatly. Calypso stared at her. *What did she mean by that?*

"You could come with me," Chiara said, answering Calypso's thought.

Calypso felt both hope and fear. "Where are you going?" she asked.

Chiara shrugged. "I don't know," she said. "Everywhere. Somewhere. I need to learn how to be a dragon. You need to learn how to be a mortal woman."

"I think you have the easier job," Calypso said, glumly.

Chiara laughed. "I think you're right," she said. She held out her hand to Calypso. "Come on," she said. "Let's seek out some brave new world together. We'll find a place where we can both learn to be free."

Calypso took her hand. Their scars touched again. "Yes," she said.

The End